GHOST PETS

By

James Wharton

D1715344

Desert Wells Publishing
Queen Creek, Arizona

James Wharton Website: jameswharton.net

Books by James Wharton

Detour
The Destiny Project
The Jaguar Queen
The Deluxe UFO Tour Company
Invasion of the Moon Women
Voyeurs
Strange Breakfast and Other Humorous Morsels
Ghost Pets
Ghosts of the Grand Canyon Country
Ghosts of Arizona's Tonto National Forest

Coming in 2013

The Destiny Project II
The Jaguar Queen II

All living creatures are bound physically and mentally by their bodies' limitations.

Death releases the soul to the spirit world where all are equal.

Antonius 103-39 BC

HEROES

Ghost Horse
(The story of Ahiga Nogana)

"In truth, few people have seen him. But some of the old people tell of the Ghost Horse. Charlie Big Hawk over at Many Farms saw him back in 1903 near Carson Mesa northwest of his house. And Billy Gonzalez from Tes Nez Iah says his grandfather saw him once over by Meridian Butte. The Ghost Horse is the combined spirit of the great warriors and brave horses of ancient times. You can see him in the rock art on the cliff walls throughout the southwest.

The horses were not here before the Spaniards came. History tells us the conquistadores brought the horses to our land. But that is the white man's history. The rock art is Indian history. It tells us the white man's history is wrong. The horse was here long before men ever came to our sacred land. Oh yes, horses were here in ancient times even before man came into this world. They were here fifteen million years ago in what the white man calls the Late Miocene period.

Indians refer to the time before man as the "time of the gods." These ancient horses were called Merychippus and were the father and mother of all the other horses. They were six feet tall and weighed one thousand pounds. But long ago,

Merychippus went away. They went away just as our people went away when they left their cliff houses and other dwellings which are all around us even now. The ancient horses and our ancestors left this land at very different times but they left for the same reason. The evil ones came from the north.

Although Merychippus would die like all other living things, his spirit remained and is with us today. It is the same for the ancient people, our ancestors. They also died but their spirits are here with us today.

Originally, our people also came from the north. The evil ones made us leave. The evil ones are not mortal men. They are ghosts and spirits that bring misfortune, sickness and death. Long ago the Sky God condemned them to prowl the Earth and witness the happiness of those who live as mortals. The Sky God makes them see the happiness they lost because of their evil deeds. But they also bring misfortune, sickness and death.

The Ghost Horse does not come here often but when he does, there is always a reason. The Ghost Horse takes two forms, pitch black or pure white. If he is black when he comes, it means evil is present and the ghosts of the north are here. He will help our people fight them.

But if he is white, all is well and everyone is safe. He comes to reassure us and remind us that his spirit is always with us."

Ahiga Nogana lay in his hospital bed listening to his grandfather Joseph Rameriz tell of the Ghost Horse.

"Will the Ghost Horse help me, Grandfather?" he asked.

"Yes, Ahiga, he will help you. He will come and make you well."

"Father," Miriam said firmly, "why do you fill his head with such nonsense? The Ghost Horse is a myth. Do not tell my child he will see the Ghost Horse. He will just be unhappy when the Ghost Horse never appears."

"It is alright, Mother," Ahiga said. "I know I am going to die. I am not afraid. But, I believe the Ghost Horse will come and I will see him."

"You see, Father," Miriam scolded Grandfather Joseph, "you see what you have done. He is hoping for something that will never happen."

With that, Miriam turned and left the room. Grandfather Joseph smiled at Ahiga.

"The young people have forgotten our beliefs, Ahiga. When you grow up, you must never forget what I have taught you. Everyone today is too busy to remember the important things. Please do not become one of those forgetful people."

"I won't, Grandfather," Ahiga said softly. "Grandfather, I don't feel so good. I heard the doctor tell Mother I would die very soon. I think it is time."

"No, Ahiga," Grandfather Joseph said, as tears began to roll on his cheeks. "Do not leave me, Ahiga. You must not die, Grandson."

The doctor and Miriam walked into the room. The doctor looked very serious and Mother was crying. Ahiga knew it was his time. The doctor nodded at Grandfather.

Grandfather Joseph smiled softly as he looked toward Ahiga. But Ahiga was grinning broadly and looking out the window. He suddenly began to laugh as he pointed toward the sky. Grandfather looked out the window and he too began to laugh. Puzzled, the doctor and Miriam looked at each other and walked over to the window.

There was only one bright cloud in the clear blue sky. It was the shining image of a great white horse triumphantly rearing up on his hind legs. The Ghost Horse had come.

Ahiga Nogana would live!

(From the short story collection *Ghosts of the Grand Canyon Country* by James Wharton)

Tibby and the Serial Killer
(The story of Eva Gregory)

A muffled thump and shattering glass frightened Eva Gregory from a deep sleep. She wasn't sure the noise was real at first, thinking, hoping she had been dreaming. But the faint screaking of hinges told her the kitchen door was slowly opening. So many times she meant to oil the hinges, but never had. Now they warned her of an intruder coming into the house.

Frozen with fear and trembling, she tried vainly to move from her bed. Even if she could, the movement risked sound. He mustn't know I'm here, she thought. But, her small one story house had two bedrooms, a dining room, living room and kitchen. He would easily find her, of course. She knew that.

She heard a slight thump as the kitchen door closed. "My god, he's in the house," she whispered. Creaking from the floor began slowly moving from the kitchen and then into the front hallway. The creaks were now advancing toward her bedroom. The intruder was moving swiftly, she thought, as if he knows where he is going. Her eyes moved to the nightstand on her right. The phone was there, but she was terrified and couldn't move her right arm to reach for it. Next to the phone was the clock. It read 1:37 A.M., the red digital numbers reflecting on the glass of the framed picture of Tibby, her beloved cat who died eight years before. She wished he was here now to comfort her and somehow protect her.

The squeaking of the floor stopped momentarily, but began again. The intruder moved a few inches, paused, then, moved again, trying to minimize the squeaking sounds from the floor. She wanted to act, to do something, but she was paralyzed with fear and could not. "Get up!" she told herself. But, it was no good. She couldn't move her terror-stricken body. She was trembling so hard she thought she would shake out of bed.

The squeaks from the floor were louder. He would be in her room soon. "He will go to the other rooms first," she thought. "I'll have time to think about what to do." She heard his steps now, right outside her door. "Oh my god!" she whispered. "Oh my god."

"He'll come to my room last," she told herself. "I need time to think."

Suddenly, her bedroom door opened. "God!" she gasped. The man stood in the doorway, silhouetted by the nightlight in the dining room. He was a big man, powerful looking. He switched on the hall light.

"Yeah Lady, you got troubles," he said. His voice was deep and his speech gruff and crude. He had come to her room first. "How did he know?" she wondered. She had no time to think but, what could she do anyway?

"Don't hurt me, please" she cried. Trying to scare him, she said, "My husband will be home any minute," she blurted. But, her voice betrayed her, revealing her fear and obvious lie.

"You ain't married, lady," the man said. "I know that 'cause I been watchin' you. I been watchin' you a long time. And, I like what I see. I know everything about you, Eva. Ha, Ha," he laughed. "Husband," he grunted. "I'm your husband tonight lady. And, you better treat me real good. You don't wanta' make hubby mad, do you? Yeah, you better not make Hubby mad," he laughed again. "You women are so dumb. I know everything about you."

"What do you want? I have no money, nothing of value. Please leave," she pleaded.

But, his reply was a perverse rhyme. "If you treat me good and make me smile, I'll let you live a little while."

"Oh my God," Eva gasped in horror. "It's you!" She suddenly realized who was standing by her bed. For the last four years, the police had searched for a serial killer murdering women in the three state area. The killer would rape them, brutally beat them, and then strangle them. He would always leave a poem at the scene of the murder. For that reason, the newspapers dubbed him the "Poet Killer."

"That's right, Eva baby. I'm the 'Poet Killer.' And it's your turn Eva. You ready to die tonight?" he laughed. "But, we'll have a little fun first. You like fun don't you, Eva?"

"Leave me alone!" she screamed.

"It always takes you girls so long to figure it out," he laughed.

"When I come callin', you're gonna be bawlin. And dead," he added. "I can't think of a rhyme for that right now. I'm thinkin' about you and me, Eva. You like my poetry?"

Eva was petrified. She knew she was going to die. It would be a horrible death.

"I'll give you everything I own," Eva whimpered. Just please don't hurt me."

"Shut up, woman. I'm gonna' take what I want anyway." The man switched on the light on Eva's nightstand. He took off his shirt and threw it on the chair. His undershirt was filthy and had holes in it. His chest and back were covered with dark hair. A heavy black beard concealed his face, but his thick lips and large, severe mouth were the features of a cruel man. He was ugly and harsh looking, here in Eva's bedroom with a purpose. He was going to rape her and kill her.

He looked down at Eva's nightstand. You got any lipstick in there, Eva? Your face is pale. Death does that to a person," he smiled. "Put on some lipstick."

Eva didn't move. Then he saw the picture of Eva's cat, Tibby. "That your cat, Eva?" he asked. "I hate cats. I used to drown them in buckets of water when I was a kid."

"It's my cat, Tibby," she said, hoping he would somehow leave if she talked to him.

"I hate cats," he said again. He grabbed the framed picture of Tibby and threw it across the room to crash against the wall.

Eva jumped as the picture shattered and fell to the floor. "Oh," she cried out, putting her hands to her mouth..

"Ha, Ha," the man laughed. "I want you to fight me Eva. You're gonna' fight me, ain't ya?" he asked.

Eva, too frightened to answer, pulled the covers up to her chin and held their edges with both hands. The man laughed again and reached down and grasped the blanket and sheet. He easily yanked them from her hands and pulled them off the bed, throwing them into the corner of the room. Eva lay trembling in her white nightgown as the man looked down at her. The look in the man's eyes terrified her. She put her arms across her breasts.

"You look even better up close, Eva" he said. "You're better lookin' than I thought." Though badly frightened, that the man had followed her added to her horror.

She suddenly bolted upward, throwing her legs to the other side of the bed. She jumped up and tried to run to the door but, the man moved quickly, and grabbed her from behind. He threw Eva back across the bed. "I like that, Eva," he said. "I like you broads to fight. It's no fun otherwise."

"You know," he continued, "the cops got it wrong. I didn't kill eleven women. I killed thirty-two by my count. They just never found the other bodies. They only find the ones I want them to find. Should I hide you, Eva, or just let them find you?"

Eva stared helplessly at the man. Strangely, she was no longer fearful, or maybe she was so numb with fear, she couldn't feel it. Anger had replaced fear. "If there was a way I could kill you, I would," she screamed.

"Yeah, I think you probably would, Eva. Too bad there ain't no way that can happen," he laughed. "I'll have my fun. You'll be dead. And, I'll go find someone else when I feel like it. Ha, Ha," he laughed, shaking his head.

"You bastard!" Eva screamed.

"That's good, Eva," he said. That's real good. I'm gonna' really enjoy this."

Then he muttered his sick rhyme. "You scream, I enjoy. Remember Eva, you're my toy."

Eva wished there was a way she could defend herself but, he was too strong, too fast. There was no way she could ever be a match for him. "You go to hell," she screamed furiously, her eyes darting, searching for an escape.

"Forget it, Eva," he said smiling. "You ain't goin' nowhere."

As the man advanced toward her, Eva glared at him. He was vulgar, evil. He killed for pleasure. Suddenly, from the corner of her eye she glimpsed movement to her left. She turned her head, desperately looking toward the end of her bed. She was shocked as she recognized a familiar sight. It was Tibby.

"Tibby," she said softly, momentarily forgetting she was going to die.

"Who you talkin' to, bitch?" he snarled. "You tryin' to play some kinda' trick on me?"

As the man reached toward Eva, Tibby leapt and landed on the killer's mid-section. Eva heard the man's undershirt shred as Tibby's claws ripped his stomach, leaving three bloody slashes. The man clutched his stomach and staggered backward from the force of the claws. "Oh god," he screamed, dropping to his knees. "How'd you do that, bitch?" he screamed, obviously not seeing Tibby. He jumped back to his feet and yelled, "I'll kill you for that."

"No you won't," Eva yelled back, looking toward Tibby.

"You're gonna' die now," he said, coming toward her quickly.

Once again Tibby sprang, landing on the killer's left shoulder. The man reached out, clawing futilely for something he couldn't see. Tibby slashed the man's face and he recoiled, tripping backward over a chair. He fell hard toward the window and its glass shattered when his head crashed through it. Enraged with pain, he leapt to his feet. He would kill the woman now.

But, something was wrong and he didn't advance toward her. As he stood by the smashed window, his right hand moved to the left side of his neck. He gasped fearfully as blood gushed from his neck with a rhythmic silence. The man screamed, knowing his wound was fatal.

"Call an ambulance," he pleaded. "Please, call an ambulance."

Eva stared coldly at him. "You go to hell." That was the last sound the man heard and he fell forward.

Tibby jumped up on the bed next to Eva. He purred softly as she stroked his back. "I knew you would come, Tibby. Somehow, I knew you would come."

As she petted Tibby, he felt softer, lighter and began to fade. "I love you, Tibby," Eva said.

And Tibby vanished like the morning mist.

Lawrence
(The story of Jerry Whitley)

Lawrence. What an odd name for a steer. I never thought about it when I was young, but as I got older, sixteen to be exact, it occurred to me how very strange it was that a one thousand pound steer would be named Lawrence. It was my uncle Frank who gave the huge animal that name. He never bothered to tell the rest of us why.

I always wondered if Lawrence knew his name was Lawrence, and if so, did he like that name? Maybe cows have their own names, I pondered, names that only other cows know.

We humans think cows are stupid. They eat too much and get fat. They're a lot like people in that respect. Maybe we humans are stupid too. When cows get fat enough, they go to the slaughter house and die. When humans get fat enough, they go to the hospital and die.

We humans eat cows like Lawrence. Cows don't eat humans, however. Maybe cows are compassionate enough to not eat humans. Maybe they are smart enough to be vegetarians. Do they know about red meat and cholesterol? I doubt if they think about such things. They are too busy enjoying the outdoors and eating grass. They probably have no idea of the gruesome fate that awaits them in a few short years. I'm not sure fat humans do either.

I didn't want to eat Lawrence. I didn't want anyone else to eat Lawrence either. Lawrence was my friend and I didn't want him to die. He won a bunch of blue ribbons for the farm. He was the state champion steer two years in a row. After accomplishing all that, he surely didn't deserve to die at the slaughterhouse and become somebody's meal.

It was at dinner one evening, however, when Uncle Frank announced Lawrence's time was at hand. He would be trucked to the slaughter house at the end of the week. The news struck me like a ton of bricks landing on my head. "We can't do that, Uncle Frank," I exclaimed, shocking everyone at the dinner table.

To farm people, Lawrence was just another animal. Yes, he'd won a lot of blue ribbons, but blue ribbons don't pay the bills. Lawrence being turned into hamburgers paid the bills. It was too awful to think about, but I couldn't get the terrible thought out of my mind. Today was Wednesday. Lawrence would be no more in just two days. "Don't take it so hard," Uncle Frank told me. "You've lived on a farm long enough to know the routine."

But it wasn't routine for me. The thought of herding the cows up the ramp into the truck and hauling them to the killing place was repulsive. It wasn't "routine" if you were a cow. It was a cruel, horrific experience. I'd only been to the killing place once. That was enough for me. I saw a cow with two broken front legs. He struggled in vain to run away on his knees with the broken halves of his front legs dragging on the ground. A fork lift drove up and pushed its steel shafts under the tortured animal's belly, hoisting the terrified animal into the air and driving away to the killing room. The animal screamed for help that would never come. It was sickening.

A stupid, evil man stuck a curved, steel hook into the horrified animal's mouth and pulled hard. The cow shrieked in agony. I never knew cows could scream, but who could blame this poor animal?

After dinner, I got up from the table and walked out to the pasture. Lawrence saw me coming and shuffled in my direction, the ground vibrating like a small earthquake with each footstep of his thousand pound body. He stopped then slowly moved closer to rub against me. "Hi Lawrence," I said. "I just got some bad news."

He moved his head and his eyes met mine. He looked sad and I wondered if he somehow already knew. But, how could he? He pressed his large body hard against mine as if he wanted to be reassured, just as a human might. That he often seemed human was a problem for me. How many times had I sat under the tree across the field and talked with Lawrence, pretending he understood as I spilled out my problems.

But, now, as he looked into my eyes, he wanted me to listen to him. He knew the brutal fate he would face in two days. I was sure of it. That's when I decided I couldn't let Lawrence die. It would be a terrible, unjust way to repay a friend. I couldn't let that happen. But, how could I save him.

Farm life was always hard. The money had been especially bad for the last few years. If Lawrence was sold for slaughter, it would bring in a lot of badly needed money. I'd get a job, I decided. They needed help at the small factory in town. I'd keep Lawrence and pay Uncle Frank more than he could get at market. That's what I'd do. It would be hard work because I also had my chores which must be done. But, I'd quit the football team and cut down my other activities.

*

It was another twelve years before Lawrence died. I fed him every day and gave him his daily pet just as I had always done. He was happy up to that day he lay down in the pasture and just went to sleep.

I missed him after he was gone. For several years, I got teary-eyed whenever I thought about him. He was a good friend and always seemed as grateful as me for our friendship.

Maybe he knew I saved his life, or at least sensed I'd done him some sort of good turn. And maybe it was my imagination. I didn't know, but I didn't care. I was just satisfied to have him with me all those years.

Several years after Lawrence died I was driving home from work as I did every day. I stopped at the sign and looked both ways before driving into the intersection. The routine day was cruelly interrupted by a powerful crashing noise and crunching of metal. My car spun round and turned over on its roof, trapping me inside. Hanging upside down, I struggled desperately to release the seat belt. But, it was hopeless. The seat belt held fast and I couldn't move.

Then the fire came. It started with a loud poof and the spilled gasoline turned the intersection into an inferno. I struggled mightily to free myself but I was doomed. "God, what an awful way to die," I shrieked. "God help me."

The flames quickly got much hotter. They were not yet inside the car but they soon would be. "Help!" I screamed. "Please help me."

But, no one came, probably because the fire raging outside the car was so hot. I hung helplessly upside down, clawing futilely at the jammed seat belt. It wouldn't open. I tried to prepare myself for the horrible death that was to quickly come.

But suddenly, the fire outside stopped. Where there had been flames there was nothing, not even smoke from the burned wreckage. Somehow, the inferno was completely extinguished. I tried to unfasten the seat belt again and it worked. I fell away from the seat, landing on the upside down ceiling of the car. As I looked out the car's windshield, I saw him, that one thousand pound steer who had always been my best friend. He stood in the roadway staring at me, just like he had so often looked at me in the past. "Lawrence," I yelled.

He lumbered over to the car as I pushed the door open. I stood up and faced him, placing my hand on his head. "Thanks buddy," I said. He moved to stand against me and I put my arms around his neck. "I miss you Lawrence," I said. He looked up at me, knowing exactly what I was saying.

"Hey buddy," a voice abruptly called from behind. "Are you okay?" the policeman asked as he ran up to me. "Who are you talking to, anyway?"

"My friend Lawrence," I said, petting his head.

"You better come over and sit down, friend," the policeman said. "You must have a concussion. There's nobody there. You're seein' things."

I smiled. There was no use telling the policeman there was a one thousand steer standing next to him.

As I held my hand on Lawrence's head, he looked up at me. His eyes were saying goodbye.

"You gotta' go, don't you Lawrence," I said, as a tears came to my eyes.

"Come on, buddy," you gotta' sit down," the policeman said. "The ambulance will be here any minute."

As I petted Lawrence's head and his large body pressed against mine, he began to fade. In seconds he was gone.

"You're a lucky guy, buddy," the policeman said. "I thought you were a goner. "Somehow, the fire went out. There's no way that could have happened, but it did. It's a miracle!" he exclaimed.

It was a miracle. But, not the kind he thought.

HAUTEUR

The Raven

"Welcome to Strawberry, Arizona," the sign said. I was just passing through, but the little town looked friendly so I decided to stop for the night. I hadn't taken a vacation for four years and this would be a well-deserved rest.

My name is Edgar Allan and I'm from Peoria, Illinois. You've probably heard of Allan's Hardware and Sundries in Peoria. It's still a family owned business after all these years. Truthfully, I can't say we stock a lot of sundries as they're too hard to keep track of but, we do have a passel of hardware. "Passel," by the way, is a literarial word I saw in a 1987 issue of the New York Literature Gazetteer which was mistakenly mailed to Ikc's Tonsorial Palace in Peoria.

Winifred Thepus' Strawberry Lodge looked exactly like an idyllic little hotel, and besides, it was the only accommodation in town. Strawberry wasn't really a town, however. It's what the Census Bureau calls a CDP, or Census Designated Place. In plain English, CDP means a concentration of population. Of course, that would describe just about any place where there were more than two people gathered.

A tall, large boned blond woman and two giddy male desk clerks who were identical twins greeted me when I walked into the small lobby of the log cabin-like building. "Good afternoon," I said.

"Welcome to our little hideaway," she smiled. "I'm Winifred Thepus. Everyone calls me Winnie."

One would think Winifred Thepus' last name was French and would likely be pronounced "they-pu" with a long "u." Or, possibly it was Hungarian and would then be snappily pronounced "thap u," again with a long "u."

But, no, things couldn't be so simple. Instead, it was pronounced "the poo."

Your last name is pronounced "the poo" as in "Winnie the Poo?" I cleverly, but mistakenly questioned.

She glared at me, and with a forced and insincere smile answered, "Yes, it is," clearly signaling she'd heard that particular attempt at humor too many times before.

"These are my sons, Billie and Bob," she continued. "My husband and I always loved the name Billie-Bob and we couldn't wait until our son was born so we could name him exactly that. But then," she added in disappointment, "I unexpectedly had twins. That messed up everything. We had to name one Billie and the other Bob. That ruined our lives. We wanted a son named Billie-Bob more than anything else in the whole world. So what happens? We get these two," she said, pointing at the twins disgustedly. "We had to split the name Billie-Bob between the likes of them," she concluded, with a resentful shrug.

The two sons, looking blatantly guilty of name theft, shifted uncomfortably and gazed downward. "She tells everyone that," Billie blurted defensively. "I never wanted to be named Billie. I'm definitely a Thaddeus, don't you think Mister Allan?" he asked, hoping to pull me into their eternal family argument.

I didn't take his bait, instead saying, "Thank you," as I took my key. I quickly walked out onto the porch and headed to room # 3. Surprisingly, the room turned out to be very nice. I went to the car to fetch my one suitcase and carried it into the spacious room. It was a comfortable place, with rustic log furniture and a nice view of the Tonto Forest out the back window. There was even a small back porch with a chair where I could sit and read while I sipped on a gin and tonic. And that's precisely what I was doing when the strangest thing happened.

I was completely engrossed in the novel when I was startled by a raspy voice calling, "Hey, you!"

I looked up but saw no one, only a large black bird perched on the log porch railing five feet from where I sat. I hadn't seen the bird land and I thought it unusual a wild bird would come so near a human. I looked around again, but saw no one.

"Hey you!" the voice called again, clearly perturbed that I hadn't answered whoever was trying to get my attention.

Again, I looked around but saw nothing.

"Over here, Bub," the voice said. "I'm over here!"

The words were coming from the direction of the large black bird which I now faced as my eyes searched for the owner of the voice.

"It's me!" the voice squawked, as the bird's beak moved concurrently with the enunciation of the words. Naturally I was astonished I was being addressed by a talking bird.

The blackbird, however, seemed to think I should take his elocutionary capability for granted. "What's wrong with you?" he asked. "You look distressed."

"Well I've never come across a talking bird before," I replied. "I did have a parakeet for a short time when I was a kid, but my mother got rid of it because it learned to curse. It used to blurt out the most awful profanity at the most inconvenient of times. Actually, it talked pretty well, although its vocabulary was limited to a few satanic but eloquent rants."

"Yeah, well, too bad about that," the black bird answered. "You humans don't treat us members of the avian community very well. You put us in cages, shoot us and eat us. Can you blame the parakeet for cussing you out?" I'd never thought about bird grievances before, but I guessed the black bird had a point. I also noticed he was a rather aloof individual.

"What do you want?" I asked, regaining my composure enough to become irritated.

"Don't pretend you don't recognize me, Mr. Edgar Allan Poe," he said firmly, suddenly becoming confrontational. "It's me, the Raven, the same one you wrote the poem about back in Baltimore. We both know you remember me. You pulled in plenty of buckos on that poem about me, but I never got a dime."

"Look, Mr. Blackbird," I replied, "My name is Edgar Allan. I own a hardware store in Peoria."

"Oh, don't pull that 'change my name' thing on me," he replied. "I wasn't hatched yesterday. You think by dropping your last name you can fool me?"

"Look, I told you, I'm not Edgar Allan Poe. My name is Edgar Allan, period."

"Oh, so now you changed your name again. You're calling yourself Edgar Allan Period instead of Edgar Allan Poe. You think you're fooling me 'cause I'm some hick bird living out here in the woods? That's dumb!"

I could see that there was no convincing this winged nutcase I wasn't Edgar Allan Poe. "Look Mr. Blackbird," I said. "I'm minding my own business and reading my book. Would you mind leaving me alone now?" I asked, hoping I could forget this improbable encounter with an escapee from the avian asylum.

"I'm afraid not, Buster," he replied mockingly. "Besides, I'm a raven, not a blackbird. Level with me. How much money did you make off our poem?" he asked.

"I'm not Edgar Allan Poe," I insisted.

"Liar, Liar!" he chided me. "You cheated me out of the money I should have gotten for our poem," the raven said. "I gave you a lot of those lines for your little masterpiece. You got all the credit and all the money. All I got were the couple pieces of stale bread you so generously threw me."

At that point, I got up to go to the office to complain. I stopped here to rest and enjoy life, not debate a deranged blackbird about a poet who died in 1849.

I walked into the office to find Winnie Thepu and her twin sons, Billie and Bob behind the desk in the exact spots they had been standing when I checked in earlier. They didn't look any happier now than they did before.

"Mrs. Thepu, Winnie," I said. "I have a small problem with my room."

"And what problem is that, Mr. Allan?" she asked.

"Well, there's this blackbird, raven I mean. He's outside on my back porch and he's talking to me. He claims he's the raven in Edgar Allan Poe's poem, 'The Raven.'"

"Have you been drinking, Mr. Allan?" she replied.

"I've had one gin and tonic but, I hardly think that qualifies as drinking in the manner you imply," I stated with great affront. As I spoke, I could see the twins, Billie and Bob giggling under their breaths.

"Look, Mr. Allan," replied Winnie. "We don't tolerate excessive imbibing in Strawberry. We are Christian people here," she proclaimed. "And, I don't buy your story about a talking raven. But," she added, "I want our guests to be happy so I'll give you another room."

The Billie and Bob twins were again looking at each other, trying hard to not burst into laughter. Bob was trying so hard not to laugh he was getting red in the face.

I soon relocated my few possessions to Room # 5, and was again sitting on the back porch reading and sipping my second gin and tonic. Just as I got comfortable and absorbed in my book, a familiar grating voice sounding like sandpaper on wood exclaimed, "I'm back. I want my money, Edgar!"

"Shoo! Get out of here!" I said, waving my arms at him. He wouldn't budge from his perch on the railing.

"I'm not leaving until we settle this thing between us," he said stubbornly.

I could see it was hopeless to chase him away and there was no use moving to yet another room. I decided it would be best to try to reason with him. "If you are really the raven from Edgar Allan Poe's famous poem," I said, "then how can you still be alive? It's 2013. Poe died one hundred and sixty-two years ago. I know a little about birds and your life span can't possibly be more than ten or fifteen years."

"Wait a minute," the raven replied. "What did you say?"

"I said, if you are the raven from the poem, you are over one hundred and sixty-two years old. Birds like don't live that long. I happen to know what I'm talking about because I'm an amateur ornithologist. We have birds in Peoria too, you know."

"No, no" the raven replied. "What year did you say it was?"

"It's 2013. Why?" I answered.

"Because if it really is 2013 and you were Edgar Allen Poe, you would look much older," he replied. "Of course, all you humans look alike," he added cynically. "Lucky for you though, we ravens are particularly intelligent. We can tell you humans apart. If it really is 2013, then you can't be Edgar Allan Poe."

"That's what I've been trying to tell you all along," I replied in exasperation. "You ravens don't listen very well," I added.

"What?" he said. "Ha, Ha. Just kidding," he cackled.

"I'm not amused," I said. I took this vacation to try and relax, not to be hassled by a deranged blackbird."

"Raven," he said. "I'm a raven. Sir, I must apologize. I have obviously mistaken you for Edgar Allan Poe. I had no idea it was 2013. One loses track of time when they're dead. My intent was to haunt Edgar Allan Poe but, alas, he predeceased me according to what you have said. I'm terribly sorry to have bothered you."

"You mean you're dead?" I asked in amazement.

"Of course, I'm dead," he replied. "Like you said, we ravens only live ten or fifteen years. I was twelve when I died."

"My God!" I exclaimed, once again astonished. "I thought I'd seen it all with a talking bird, raven, I mean. But, a dead talking raven, now that takes the cake," I replied.

"Look Mister Allan, I apologize again for any inconvenience I've caused. I shall leave you now, never to return."

"You'll not return to haunt me anymore?" I asked hopefully.

"Nevermore," quoth the raven. Then, he slowly faded into nothingness, leaving me staring into the trees.

I went into my room and fixed myself another gin and tonic. "I've been haunted by Edgar Allan Poe's raven," I said proudly, as if I had accomplished some remarkable feat.

"Nevermore," a deathly voice eerily whispered.

(From the short story collection *Ghosts of Arizona's Tonto National Forest* by James Wharton)

Ghostly Discomfitures on Grand Canyon Road

Horribly embarrassing! That's what it was. It was horribly embarrassing to try and explain how I fell out of my car on the entrance road of Grand Canyon National Park. To make matters worse, the car, my pride and joy and now devoid of occupants, continued traveling down the road for exactly four and one third more miles.

That was the distance the insurance company determined the empty vehicle travelled before driving itself off the south rim of the Grand Canyon in a self-destructive plunge of eight hundred and fifty two feet. The insurance company also measured that distance, but I don't know why exactly.

Not a technical person, in my dark imaginings I suspected disgruntled mechanical paraphernalia underneath the automobile's hood concocted a vehicular suicide pact to avenge my not changing the oil or some other transgression. Of course, I hadn't planned on my car arriving at my destination several hours before me nor that in the seconds before its fatal dive it would create a scene driving past horrified on-lookers enjoying afternoon cocktails on the patio of the Bright Angel Lodge. As it turned out, they all figured the car was full of people.

But, I soon learned my suspicions regarding the car's committing suicide were incorrect. In truth, the car's unsettling demise was the work of unearthly forces. Here is why I think that.

After falling out of the car, as I lay there in the road watching it disappear I suddenly felt a sense of unease, as if I were being watched. I nervously got to my feet and looked around. Tall, dark green pine forests lined each side of the road. The trees did not stand close together but were loosely spaced approximately fifteen feet from each other. This allowed me to look into the forests seventy-five or so feet.

Although I saw nothing, I heard voices. The sounds of the breeze blowing through the tall pines were actually moans and whispers. Don't think for a moment that trees can't talk because I heard them clearly. The trees had taken note of my less than fortunate circumstances and were discussing my plight. It was none too flattering.

"Did you see that guy fall out of his car?" one of the trees said.

"Did you ever see anything so dumb in your life, Gerald?"

From the conversation, it was obvious the pine tree just off the dusty road and to my left was named Gerald. He knew I was watching him closely so he wisely chose not to answer that question posed by the catty female pine tree who naturally did not identify herself. For some reason, I thought her name might be Helen.

"Mister, you sure chose the wrong time and place to fall out of your car," a raspy voice behind me said.

I spun round to find myself facing a three-foot tall turkey vulture or buzzard as some call them. I was becoming a bit unnerved. It was one thing to encounter talking trees. I could rationalize that peculiarity by blaming the wind and an overactive imagination. But, a talking buzzard was more than my badly rattled nerves could handle. "What kind of buzzard are you?" I replied, as I stared at the ghastly looking creature. I was not comforted by my sudden remembrance that buzzards are always associated with death and hauntings in the movies.

"I ain't a buzzard," was the indignant reply. "I'm a turkey vulture, but, you can call me a buzzard, if you like."

"Well, whatever," I said. "You go around eating dead animals so I don't think I'd be too particular about what I'm called."

"I don't eat dead animals," he shot back. "I'm a vegetarian."

"You're a vegetarian vulture?" I asked in amazement. Now I've seen it all, I thought.

"How is it you can talk?" I asked, still deeply distressed that he could. It turned out to be a longer story than I wanted to hear.

"On this exact date in 1883 I was riding shotgun on the Williams to Grand Canyon Stage Coach. There was only me and the driver, a mean hombre named "Nasty" Percival Montague. "Nasty" was not his given name, of course. There warn't no passengers, just Nasty Percival and me. We was haulin' mail and some packages but most important, we was carryin' four cases of whiskey. Me and Nasty Percival could absolutely not help ourselves and we opened a wooden case and each pulled out a bottle. We was drunk in no time."

Although I found the talking buzzard incredible and his story unbelievable, I stood and listened to him ramble on.

"It warn't too long before Nasty Percival and me got into a fight. He threw me off the stage as it was flying down the road and I landed just about where you did when you fell out of your velocipede (aka automobile). Without bothering to rein in the horses and stop, he jumped up on top the stage coach and screamed and cussed at me wavin' his bottle in one hand and his hat in the other, laughin' and carryin' on like Judgement Day was upon us."

"That still doesn't answer my question about how you can talk," I said.

"I'm gettin' to it, Mister," he said. "You're danged impatient."

"Sorry. It's just that I find your story captivating."

"Capti-what?" the vegetarian vulture said.

"Never mind," I replied. "Please, get on with it."

"Anyway, as Nasty Percival stood on top of the stage coach and screamed obscenities and laughed at me, something awful happened. I tried to warn him but he was too drunk and when I waved and yelled at him to duck down, he just got even more worked up and hollered and cussed at me even louder. That's when the coach went under a tree branch that knocked Nasty Percival's head clean off. It went bouncing into the ditch up the road about two hundred yards from here."

"Oh my lord," I said. "Where did you bury the poor man?"

"Well, that's the thing. The stagecoach kept rollin' and his body kept wavin' and curses were comin' out the collar of his shirt which is where he now poured his whiskey into. It was a awful sight. I run up the road to get his head for him but I got the gol darndest surprise instead. His head was layin' in the mud and facin' me see. And suddenly, the eyes opened wide and the head said, 'Where's Nasty?'"

"That must have scared you mightily," I replied, still not accepting the outlandish reality of listening to a talking buzzard describe his conversation with the bodiless head of a drunken stagecoach driver.

"Oh, it did for sure, Mister. So I says to the head, I'll take you with me and we'll find Nasty."

'Oh no you won't,' the head says." 'I don't like Nasty so I'll just venture out on my own. I'm gonna' quit while I'm ahead,' it says, tryin' to be funny."

"And then the head flew off in the opposite direction. That would be to the south," the turkey vulture said, looking down the road behind him.

"Anyways," the vulture continued, "I was left stranded here and somehow fell in with some Indians havin' a peyote party. You know, peyote is a drug that comes from the peyote cactus. Anyway, I was already drunk and once I got into the peyote, I don't remember nothin."

"The next morning I woke up next to a very nice Indian lady with no teeth and seventeen kids. 'We're married,' she says. "But, I can't be married, I says. I already got me a wife. Well, as luck would have it, this was the mother of the tribe's medicine man. He got very upset with me and turned me into a turkey vulture, or buzzard as you say, which I've been ever since. That's how I can talk. I used to be a human before I died."

"You mean you're a ghost on top of being a talking vulture?" I asked, now horrified.

"I'm afraid so," he said. "This all happened over a hundred years ago. What do you expect?"

"What do you want with me?" I asked.

"I want you to adopt me and take me home. You can tell everyone I'm a new species of parrot. They'll never know I'm really a deceased buzzard that used to be a human. Besides, I need a place to stay."

"My friends will never believe you're a parrot," I said. "They'll all know you're a buzzard and they'll laugh at me."

"They'll believe you," the buzzard said. "You don't look that smart so your friends can't be that smart either. How about it? We got a deal?"

I took off running as fast as I could. I never ran four and one-third miles before, but I got to the Bright Angel Lodge just before last call for afternoon cocktails. It was late in October and the sun was already sinking low in the western sky. Darkness would soon be upon us.

As I sat there sipping my martini and listening to people tell me about the car full of people that rolled off the rim and fell into the canyon earlier, I spied that turkey vulture standing on the roof of the lodge watching every move I made. I had a sense of deep apprehension. For no good reason, my eyes wandered toward the window of my room. I was horrified to see a ghastly, phantom-like, disembodied head glaring back at me. I was praying the headless driver and his stagecoach and would not also arrive.

From behind me, someone suddenly put a hand on my right shoulder. A strong odor of horses and cheap whiskey filled the air. Trembling in horror, I dared not turn around.

A deathly, hollow voice turned my blood to ice. "The stagecoach is here for you, Mister. Of course, if you adopt the buzzard, you won't have to take the stagecoach ride."

That's how I ended up with the ghost of a deceased buzzard who used to be human. Oh, I never told you how I happened to fall out of my car. No, I surely didn't. But, that's another story.

(From the short story collection *Ghosts of the Grand Canyon Country* by James Wharton)

Hip-Hop

Jack Dhaltry, the CEO of Tremaine Global Finance Ltd, stood at the far end of the conference table as he called the meeting to order. "I got a ten o'clock tee time, gentlemen," he said with a smile, "so this is going to be a short meeting. I talked with Dohrnberg Investment Bank late yesterday and committed to selling five billion worth of prime mortgage bonds. We go sell 'em to the municipal pension funds just like before. Remember how much money we made on those deals."

With the exception of one man, Kevin Ellison, there were unanimous smiles and an enthusiastic round of applause around the long conference table. Like everyone else at the table, Ellison knew Wall Street's last round of A+ rated financial products were actually worthless investments causing millions of people to lose their pensions and life savings.

Ellison, a regional sales manager, had long been a thorn in Jack Dhaltry's side. Although Ellison was one of the company's top sales producers, he balked at selling risky financial products to pension funds of cities and businesses.

Ellison would be a natural to replace Jack Dhaltry as CEO if he didn't have a conscience. Unfortunately, he did.

When Dhaltry saw Kevin Ellison's unenthusiastic response to the new, highly profitable products from Dohrnberg Investment Bankers, he decided he had enough. "What the hell is your problem this time, Kevin?" he asked in a belligerent tone.

Kevin Ellison knew this day would come. The CEO was challenging him because he didn't approve of the company selling high risk financial instruments to pension funds and representing them as safe investments.

"It's my usual concern, Jack." Kevin replied. "This stuff is crap and we all know it. The last several batches of this Wall Street junk were garbage. Wall Street took positions on the junk they gave us knowing it would fail. Wall Street and Tremaine Global made fantastic money, but the pension funds went broke and thousands of people were left with no retirement income."

"I'm tired of your holier than though nonsense, Kevin. We operate the way the world operates. It's dog eat dog out there. If you weren't one of my top sales managers, I'd fire you."

"People lost their houses, Jack. They had to try and find work at age seventy just to put food on their table. They depended on us for a secure retirement and look what we did to them. Doesn't that bother anyone but me? It's a horrible thing we did. Once again, you're asking us to sell financial products that are sure to fail. That's fraud, Jack. We make a lot of money by bankrupting thousands of people who rely on us to protect their investments."

"Kevin, this is a sales meeting. Our guys are pumped to go out and make lots of money. You're raining on our parade."

"You don't have to fire me, Jack. I quit. I can't do this anymore," Kevin said, as he got up to walk out of the conference room.

"Good riddance," Jack laughed, as the twenty-nine remaining regional sales managers watched Kevin walk through the door.

The conference room was separated from the general office by a glass partition. Approximately one hundred employees worked at desks in the general office on the other side of the conference room's glass wall. They also watched Kevin as he walked out of the meeting. They knew exactly what had happened. As Kevin walked past, they gave him supportive winks and smiles. He was a man of principles. Unfortunately, he was now unemployed.

The employees in the general office had watched the whole thing. They knew a confrontation between Kevin Ellison and Jack Dhaltry had been brewing. They would miss Kevin and they disliked Dhaltry immensely. They continued to work at their desks, periodically glancing up at the men on the other side of the conference room's glass wall to see "what was going on." Of course, all they could do is get a general impression of things by looking at the expressions on the men's faces. The meeting continued.

"Okay, people," Dhaltry said, "let's get back to making money." Everyone nodded in agreement. "Yeah," the group replied smiling.

Jack Dhaltry was standing at the end of the table as he distributed the packages of complex financial products his team would carry to market. Dhaltry and his team knew the more complex the financial instruments were the harder they were for pension fund and company managers to understand and analyze. That made the products easier to sell because the answers Tremaine Global sales representatives provided were also complex. Like sheep going to slaughter, the customers purchasing these products shook their heads yes, only pretending to understand what they had been told.

Once everyone had received the promotional package, a smiling Jack Dhaltry looked at the group and prepared to speak. But, there was silence as a perplexed expression abruptly appeared on Dhaltry's face. "What the hell are you?" he yelled, as he stared defiantly toward the other end of the conference table.

Perplexed and shocked, the twenty-nine regional sales managers sitting at the table looked at each other in bewilderment. Who is Jack talking to, they wondered.

"Is this someone's idea of a joke?" he asked. "It's not funny. I've already fired one man this morning. Whoever put that thing on the conference table better get it off there right now."

Again, the regional sales managers looked at each other wondering what was going on.

"Get that thing off the conference room table," Jack Dhaltry screamed. "Whoever put it there is going to be out of a job in about three seconds."

Finally, one of the twenty-nine managers spoke. "Jack, what are you talking about?"

Dhaltry looked at Sam Needham, a man he thoroughly trusted. "Are you in on this, Sam?" he asked.

"Jack, I'm sorry, but none of us know what you're talking about. What's going on?"

Dhaltry believed Sam Needham. "Sam," he answered, "are you guys playing a joke on me or do you truly not see that kangaroo wearing a trench coat and holding a shotgun standing in the middle of the table two feet from where you're sitting?"

Everyone looked around the table, empty except for the financial products packages from Wall Street. "Are you playing a joke on us, Jack?" Sam replied. "There's nothing on the table but the brochures you just gave us."

Jack Dhaltry stared at the group, speechless for the first time in his life. "They can't see me, Jack," the creature said. "They can't hear me either."

"What did you say?" Dhaltry yelled, seemingly looking at Ed Chesley sitting at the far end of the table.

"I didn't say anything, Jack," the alarmed Chesley replied.

"No, not you," Dhaltry screamed, "that thing standing in front of you.

The twenty-nine dismayed sales managers wondered if Jack Dhaltry had lost his mind or had a stroke. "Jack," Sam Needham said, "do you feel alright? None of us see anything on the table except the financial product brochures."

"Are you people telling me you don't see a kangaroo with a shotgun standing on the conference table? Chesley, stick your hand out. He's right there in front of you."

Ed Chesley slowly reached forward as Jack directed. "Jack, for god's sake. There's nothing there," he said, convincing Dhaltry his team wasn't playing tricks on him. He looked back at the gun-toting marsupial standing at the other end of the table.

"My name is Octavia Henderson," the kangaroo said. "I'm a hit lady, as in I kill people," she said. "Oh, and by the way, I'm a ghost. I died when one of those so called highly rated financial instruments you sell collapsed and put our town into bankruptcy. They closed the zoo and euthanized us because no other zoos could afford to take us. Their cities bought some of your worthless products also."

"You're a kangaroo hit lady?" Dhaltry laughed. "And you kill people? You have got to be kidding me. Did you hear that, people?"

Sam Needham got up from his chair and walked to the conference room door, convinced that his boss Jack Dhaltry had a stroke or some kind of mental breakdown. But, as he grasped the door handle, he discovered it was locked. He again tried to turn the handle to open the door. It wouldn't budge.

"Tell Sam to sit down, Jack," the kangaroo said sternly. "The little town that hired me, one of many you bankrupted, doesn't want me to kill you. They want me to punish you and your cohorts for making everyone's lives so miserable. They want your lives to be miserable too and that's why I'm here."

"Sit down, Sam," Dhaltry said. He turned to Octavia. "What the hell do you want?" he asked, thinking the overbearing kangaroo hit lady reminded him of his father.

"I want you and your twenty-nine minions here to open your financial products brochures and pull out the two sheets at the front, just inside the cover."

"Men," Jack said, "I know you think I've gone nuts, but play along with me for a few minutes until I sort this thing out. Open your brochures and pull out the first two sheets." The men looked at Jack with blank stares, but did as he instructed.

"Okay, kangaroo hit lady," he said. "What now?"

"I prefer to be called Octavia, Jack. Octavia is so much more civilized than 'hit lady,' don't you think."

"Whatever," Jack answered scornfully.

"There are five places marked with a red X where they must sign their names," Octavia said. "And, I don't like your attitude, Jack. Have you no respect for women?"

"You're a kangaroo with a shotgun and wearing a trench coat. I don't think that's very lady-like," Dhaltry responded.

"That was hurtful, Jack. You best be careful not to rile a lady." Dhaltry didn't reply.

"Okay, Jack," Octavia said, "you and your men sign your names where indicated by the five red X's on the papers you're holding."

"Can't we read them first?" Dhaltry asked.

"No," Octavia answered. "You never have your clients read anything first. Even if they did, there's so much fine print there's really no point in their trying to understand them or what they are signing. Now sign," Octavia demanded assertively.

Dhaltry looked at the two sheets of paper. "This is a power of attorney giving you control of Tremaine Global's Assets and all my personal assets," Dhaltry said. "Did you hear what I just said, people? This crazy kangaroo is telling me to have everyone in this room surrender all their assets to her." The twenty-nine sales managers laughed. They couldn't see the invisible kangaroo, but each of them played along with Dhaltry because that's what everyone else everyone else was doing.

"I thought that would be your response, Jack," Octavia said. "The money is not for me. It's going to be returned to the pension fund of the small town that hired me. Like I said, they are bankrupt thanks to you and your henchmen. But now, I'm going to give you a lesson in humility so you will learn how to be more obedient. Take off all your clothes, Dhaltry," Octavia ordered, her tone becoming confrontational.

"She wants me to strip, guys," Dhaltry laughed toward the group. The group forced a few chuckles, still wondering what was happening with their boss.

Suddenly, a sharp pain in Jack's rear-end caused him to scream, startling everyone at the conference table. "Strip now," Octavia ordered, and a second stabbing feeling shot through Dhaltry's buttocks. "Ouch!" he exclaimed, grasping his behind and falling to the floor. He got back up and immediately tore off his clothes and shoes and stood naked before the group.

A low murmur buzzed among the one hundred employees in the outer office as they began looking up from their computers toward the conference room. They wondered why their leader was naked.

"Tell them to sign their forms, Jack," Octavia ordered.

"They won't sign anything giving you all their assets," Jack responded combatively. "And, either will I."

Another horrific pain shot through Dhaltry's rear-end and he fell to the floor screaming, "My ass is on fire."

"What you're feeling, Dhaltry, is a pain in the ass."

"I know that, lady," he replied.

"But, you don't understand Jack and it's so important that you do. You see, the proverbial pain in the ass is much more than just a feeling of discomfort. It is an actual thing, an ethereal object that certain chosen people, kangaroos in my

40

case, can control. I can deliver the proverbial pain in the ass to you in measured portions, increasing the intensity of the hurt to the point where your butt will actually feel like it is being torn off. But that is so vulgar and bloody, wouldn't you say. I am hopeful you will walk out of this room today with your posterior intact, Jack. But, that is entirely up to you. Tell all of your men to strip completely and pile all their clothes and shoes in the back corner of the room."

An intimidated Jack Dhaltry ordered the twenty-nine men to strip and put their clothes in a pile. To a man, they refused. Suddenly, twenty-nine more kangaroos holding shotguns appeared in the room. But, these kangaroos were completely visible to the twenty-nine regional sales managers, as was Octavia. Each kangaroo stood next to one of the men. "Hi, I've been assigned to you," each of them announced to their respective sales manager. "Strip," they ordered their manager. The more stubborn of the managers who refused to take off their clothes suffered the same searing pain in their hind ends as Jack Dhaltry felt. Within minutes they were all naked.

None of the high powered sales managers in the room felt nearly as confident as they had before. They were humbled and very nervous. Something was happening here that they couldn't understand and it wasn't good. The one hundred employees in the outer office gazed at the nude men with great interest. What the heck kind of sales meeting is that, they wondered. They noticed that all the men were signing sheets of paper. Little did they know, the men had just signed away all their assets to Octavia Henderson, kangaroo hit lady. Octavia and the other twenty-nine shotgun wielding kangaroos in the room were invisible to the people in the outer office.

"Alright, you men," Octavia declared. "You are going to be punished for stealing money from all those innocent people over the years. You ruined their lives and you will now pay the price. Your punishment is this. For the rest of your lives, you are condemned to be human kangaroos. You must hold your arms up and let your hands hang and hop around like a kangaroo. That will remind you of the thieves you are and our lovely time together today. Let me see you practice that kangaroo posture and your hop. The intimidated men started hopping around, holding their hands in front of their chests.

"That is very good, gentlemen," Octavia said. "Of course, you don't look nearly as good as real kangaroos. Now hear this. Any time you don't act in the kangaroo way, the proverbial pain in the ass will shoot through your rear end. You see, your personal kangaroo will accompany you every moment for the rest of your lives. If you stop acting like a kangaroo for even one second, you get the pain in your back side. Everybody now, let's hop!" Octavia said enthusiastically.

All thirty of the men in the room began hopping around as they held their arms up like kangaroos. As the thirty naked men hopped around the room, the one hundred outer office employees stared in wonder.

"What are they doing in there?" a woman asked.

"It's a new team building exercise," a man answered authoritatively. "Watch, they'll probably do that stupid trust-fall next. I'm glad I'm not a manager."

HAUNTERS

The Possession of JoJo the Toy Monkey

JoJo, the squeezable, stuffed monkey sat on the edge of the desk gazing sadly across the patient consultation room. His enormous blue plastic eyes looked directly into Marian's as she lay on the couch waiting for Dr. Collier to begin today's session. The little brown monkey's unhappy expression reminded Marian of someone with whom she had been involved before she married Howard. Marian tried to avoid looking into JoJo's eyes but, she couldn't stop staring at him. Who does that monkey remind me of? she wondered. "Stop looking at me you little weirdo!" she exclaimed silently. But, JoJo's blue plastic eyes were fixed, peering into her very soul.

Although a child's toy, JoJo functioned as the "positivity motivator" at the Collier Center for Mental Wellness. Kimberley, Dr. Collier's blonde, intellectually dim intern, used JoJo to reward patients whenever they achieved a pre-determined mental goal. When JoJo's tummy was squeezed, his little red hat moved up and down and his little tin cymbals banged together three times. At first, Marian thought it was a stupid reward, but she soon found herself coming to each session desperately hoping JoJo would celebrate her progress. When she failed to be rewarded at her prior session, she found herself depressed the entire week, wondering why the brown toy monkey didn't bang his cymbals and raise his little red hat three times. Marian found JoJo creepy, but craved his approval. God, I am nuts, she thought. But, she couldn't help herself.

Marian had taken an instant dislike to Kimberley when she first met her at the session four weeks earlier. The young intern's long legs and ridiculously gorgeous figure immediately upset Marian. That only Kimberley was allowed to squeeze JoJo also perturbed her.

But, that wasn't all. Marian suspected it was more than mere coincidence that Kimberley's large blue eyes and forlorn, empty stare resembled JoJo's. She feared the slithering blonde and toy monkey had formed an unnatural alliance and were conspiring against her. That both Kimberley and JoJo opted out when brains were distributed reinforced her suspicions.

"Alright Marian," Dr. Collier said, "we'll begin today's session. Are you ready, JoJo?" he asked.

"Yes I am, Dr. Collier," answered Kimberley, pretending to speak in JoJo's voice. Laughing gleefully, she squeezed JoJo's tummy and his red hat went up and down and his cymbals clinked. "Analysis is so fun!" she shrieked.

For some reason, maybe because Dr. Collier couldn't stop looking at Kimberley's legs, Marian concluded Kimberley functioned as more than just his intern. JoJo also appeared to be leering at Kimberley's legs, his sad look seemingly replaced by a lustful expression. "It's almost as if he's alive," thought Marian, "and just as horny as all other men."

Marian looked closely at JoJo. He reminds me of somebody but, I just can't place him, she again pondered.

"Today is hypno-therapy day, Marian," Dr. Collier announced. "Are you ready for hypno-therapy, JoJo?" he asked. Kimberley squeezed JoJo and his little hat went up and down and his cymbals clinked. "Oh, I'm so ready, Dr. Collier," Kimberley squealed in JoJo's pretend voice. Marian was hypnotized within seconds.

To this day, Marian never figured out exactly what happened next. She suddenly found herself awake, no longer hypnotized. Kimberley and Dr. Collier were not in the room and only Marian and JoJo remained. She was still lying on the couch however JoJo was now standing on Marian's chest and looking down into her eyes.

"Get off of me you freak!" she screamed, at the now smiling monkey.

"Don't you remember me, Marian?" he asked, with a sinister grin.

"No, I don't remember you!" Marian yelled in alarm. "How can a toy monkey be talking?"

"I'm your Basset Hound, Clyde, the one you trained to hold his rear end up in the air when he went to the bathroom. That was real funny, Marian. I was doing my best to please you and do just like you said when I urinated. I raised both my rear legs high in the air and relieved myself just like you trained me to do. All you did was laugh at me. Then you got the neighbors laughing at me. You humiliated me, Marian. And now, it's payback time."

"How can you be Clyde, my dumb Basset Hound? You're JoJo the monkey," Marian said.

"I died, Marian, remember?" Clyde answered. "I died of humiliation. But, I'm back as a ghost and I've taken possession of JoJo's inanimate body. He doesn't have a brain, you know, so it wasn't that hard."

"My god," Marian said, "you really are Clyde the Basset Hound. Get out of here, Clyde, you high altitude pisser," Marian demanded, laughing cruelly.

"Unless you've got a resident exorcist handy, I'll be with you for a while," Clyde-JoJo responded. "I'm gonna' get even with you, Marian."

Marian tried to get up. It was then she realized she was tied to the couch. "Turn me loose, you dead little creep," she demanded, becoming frightened.

Clyde-JoJo's red hat went up and down and his cymbals banged together. "Not a chance, Marian," he replied. "You got any idea how hard it is for a Basset Hound to simultaneously raise his hind legs skyward and pee? It's real hard, Marian. I threw my back out so many times I lost count. I can't count that well anyway."

"What do you want with me, Clyde-JoJo?" Marian asked, tension apparent in her voice.

"I want to haunt you, Marian," he answered. "I want to scare the bejeebers out of you for starters."

"What the hell is a bejeeber?" asked Marian, thinking it might be a physical object that the Basset Hound possessed monkey might somehow extract from her body.

Clyde-JoJo thought about that for a moment. "I don't rightly know," he answered. "But, you'll be scared, just the same."

"You don't scare me you Clyde-JoJo thing," Marian said, challenging the Basset Hound ghost. "A possessed toy monkey doesn't scare me," she added. But, it really did.

"Oh yeah," replied Clyde-JoJo. "Watch this," he said. Suddenly, Clyde-JoJo's possessed monkey body started jumping up and down on Marian's chest and banging his cymbals in her face. For some reason, his little red hat didn't go up and down as it usually did when his cymbals banged. That also scared Marian. Then, Clyde-JoJo started barking. Marian had never seen a barking toy monkey with blue plastic eyes and her anxiety level climbed ever higher. JoJo started snarling at her. That terrified her.

"Don't you snarl at me Clyde-JoJo or whoever you are," demanded Marian, putting up a brave front. She was worried the Basset Hound possessed monkey jumping up and down on her chest was going to bite her on the nose.

"I'm gonna bite you on your nose, Marian," Clyde-JoJo said, speaking in a scary, ghostly tone and confirming her fears.

"Help! Help!" Marian screamed.

"Clyde-JoJo laughed. "No one can hear you, Marian. Lookee what I'm gonna' do next!" he exclaimed joyfully, as he stopped jumping on Marian's chest. He walked over to her chin and bent forward slightly. "Want a little kiss, Marian?" he asked.

"Get away from me!" she shrieked.

"Ha, Ha. I don't want to kiss you anyway. But, look what you're missing," he added. Suddenly, Clyde-JoJo's head rotated three hundred and sixty degrees, turning around completely.

"Oh my god!" Marian screamed. "Help! Help!" she cried.

Clyde-JoJo jumped from Marian's chest, scampered across the floor and hopped up on Dr. Collier's desk. "Aghhh!" he screamed, and a streaming arc of black ink spewed from his mouth and over to the couch and Marian. In seconds, Marian's dress was soaked with the black fluid. She was screaming as loudly as she could but, no help came.

Clyde-JoJo jumped from the desk onto a nearby table, knocking a lamp to the floor. Clyde-JoJo started throwing books, computers, vases and anything else he could see. Then he turned over chairs and other office furniture, quickly trashing the entire office.

Marian was completely terrified and still screaming.

"Marian, Marian," she heard a voice yell. Someone was shaking her arm. "Marian, wake up. It's Dr. Collier. Wake up, Marian," he said.

"Oh my god!" Marian exclaimed, as Dr. Collier and Kimberley suddenly appeared sitting next to the couch on which Marian lay. "Thank goodness you're here," she yelled in relief. "Your little monkey's trying to kill me!"

"What on earth are you talking about, Marian?" Dr. Collier asked in amazement.

"JoJo was standing on my chest and was trying to kill me. My Basset Hound Clyde is possessing JoJo's body and he's wrecking the office. He's going to kill me, Doctor," she insisted.

48

"Calm down, Marian," Dr Collier said. There's nothing wrong with the office. Everything's fine. No one's trying to kill you. Our hypno-therapy session must have gone badly. It happens from time to time. We'll do better next week, I promise, Marian," he said.

Marian, still shaking, looked around the office. Everything was in order. There was no turned over furniture or broken lamp. JoJo stood in his customary place on Dr. Collier's desk. Everything appeared to be normal, but Marian was still very upset.

"Look, Marian," Dr. Collier said, as he stood up, "I'm going to prescribe some tranquilizers. You need to relax. You're imagining things. Take some time off from work and rest. You're a nervous wreck."

"Marian, now slightly more composed, said, "Alright, Dr. Collier."

"Kimberley will stay with you for a moment. I left my prescription pad in the next office," Dr. Collier said, as he walked through the door.

Kimberley smiled at Marian. "Let me hold your hand, Marian. You'll feel better," she said, taking Marian's right hand.

"Alright, Kimberley," Marian answered, as she looked toward the woman. "Her blue eyes look just like JoJo's," she thought to herself.

"Yes, they do, don't they Marian," Kimberley answered.

Marian gasped, as a satanic smile came across Kimberley's face. "How did you know what I was thinking?" Marian asked fearfully.

Suddenly, long, drooping, Basset Hound ears hung at the sides of Kimberley's head. Marian recoiled in shock and screamed. Kimberley's head rotated completely around and black ink shot from her mouth and all over Marian. Marian tried to get up and run but, she couldn't move. She could only scream in terror.

The office door flew open and Dr. Collier came running into the office. "What is it, Marian," he asked. "What's wrong with you?"

"It's Kimberley!" Marian shrieked. "Kimberley is a dead Basset Hound and she's trying to kill me."

Dr. Collier looked over at Kimberley who was sitting calmly and shaking her head. Marian got up and ran out of the office.

"What's with her?" he asked Kimberley. Kimberley got up and walked over to Dr. Collier. "Forget about her, Baby," she purred. "She's too crazy for us to cure."

Dr. Collier smiled. "I think we need a private consultation, Kimberley," he winked. He turned and walked across the room to shut the door.

Kimberley's head rotated completely around and an evil smile came across her face. JoJo, the squeezable, stuffed monkey sat on the edge of the desk gazing across the patient consultation room. He was smiling.

Bad Weather

Randy Gibson stared upward at the sienna rock walls towering three thousand feet above him. "Incredible, isn't it," he remarked to his hiking partner, Mike Weber.

"Yeah," Mike said, I'm amazed every time we come down here.

The two men had just descended three thousand feet down a south rim back country trail in the Grand Canyon. Although the main canyon trails are well marked and easy to follow, the back country trails often fade into nothingness, leaving the inexperienced hiker confused and sometimes lost.

Randy and Mike were experienced hikers however, and had been down this trail many times in the past. Even so, they always made it a point to choose a landmark for a reference point in case they found themselves wandering too far off the trail. The landmark they always used was the perpendicular black stain on the large cliff behind them.

The stain, which was approximately five hundred feet in length, was made by eons of water flowing down the vertical cliff face. On their descent, they had followed the trail's many switchbacks which wound around the side of the cliff and they were now at its base taking a short break.

As the two men looked at the rim of the cliff high above them, they noticed dark clouds in the northeastern sky. Wide sheets of thick rain resembled stationary gray curtains hanging from the leaden clouds. The downpour was already soaking the parched plains at the top of the canyon's south rim. While the sky had been clear when they began their hike less than two hours earlier, things had changed quickly.

"Thunderstorm," Mike remarked. Both men knew that meant trouble. The hard desert floor would only absorb an insignificant amount of the large volume of water abruptly dumped on it. The bulk of the water would be run-off, a liquid sheet flowing over the desert's hard earth and seeking the lowest point. Eventually, the water would reach the low points which were the dry streambeds.

Because of the massive volume of water generated by an intense thunderstorm such as this, the streambeds would immediately fill and the water would cascade downward still seeking the lowest point. However, as the distance the water flowed downward increased, the faster the water travelled, soon becoming a raging deluge reaching incredible speeds, a wall of water with massive force. It would become a flash flood looking for a place to happen.

Although Randy and Mike were still on a high trail, random washes crossed the trail ahead. Even though it wasn't raining directly above them, these washes would also fill with water and send an angry wall of water crashing downward. They would have to be extra cautious on the trail before them.

Oddly, in the next hour of hiking, the dry creeks crossing the trail had remained dry. They never had a drop of rain during their hike. They followed the trail as it curved around a one hundred foot high rock, expecting to see the deep gorge that always greeted them when the trail straightened out. Instead, they were shocked because in place of the gorge was a wide lake.

"Unbelievable," Randy gasped.

"Where'd that lake come from?" Mike asked, although both men immediately realized what had happened.

The one hundred foot deep gorge was the low point where many of the streambeds in this section of the canyon converged. The heavy thunderstorm had produced an enormous amount of water which poured into the streambeds which eventually poured into the gorge. Mike and Randy had been to the bottom of the gorge via a trail with steep switchbacks which ran down its side. They also knew that a wide, deep streambed on the floor of the gorge normally carried water out of it. However, this streambed went through a large, cave-like hole under the rocks on the gorge's north side. This natural drain pipe was carved in the bottom of the rocks by eons of rainstorms. This water would then flow downward to the ultimate low point, the Colorado River, still over four thousand feet further below them. Today, however, the streambed didn't carry the water away. Instead, water accumulated in the gorge, quickly filling it and creating a lake one hundred feet deep and two hundred feet wide. That was the sight at which the two men now gazed.

What had happened was typical of thunderstorm events such as this. As water flows across the flatter land and into the streambeds, it collects debris such as branches, logs and plants. As this debris is pushed along, it can get jammed up at turns or narrow spots in the streambeds. If there is enough debris, it can form a dam which blocks the water and forms a lake. The huge volume of debris carried by the water from this storm accumulated in the large natural drain hole in the bottom of the gorge's north wall, thus creating a natural dam. With nowhere to flow, the water rapidly accumulated in the gorge and a temporary lake was formed.

Eventually, of course, the dam will break and send an explosion of water crashing down the streambed catching the unwary by surprise. The large lake would disappear in minutes or less. Because of its immense size, this lake created an exceedingly dangerous situation.

"We gotta' tell the rangers about this," Mike said. "This is a killer flash flood waiting to happen. There's a huge amount of water in there."

"I know," Randy replied, but our cell phones don't have reception until we get another thousand feet back up the canyon. I'm looking at something else," he added, as he looked at the small canyon directly across the newly formed lake.

"No way," Mike said. "The only way to get there is to swim the two hundred feet across that water."

"So," Randy said, "let's go."

"You're nuts," Mike said. "If we're in that lake when that dam gives way, we're dead. You know that. Come on, man. That's stupid."

"Mike," Randy snapped, "we've always wanted to go over there and explore that little canyon but we could never get there. Now is the chance we've been waiting for. Let's go for it. The dam will hold."

"Maybe," Mike said, weakening. "But, what if we're over there in the canyon when the dam bursts? We'll be trapped. There's no way back across or down. It's a sheer drop-off of at least one hundred feet."

"We'll find a way out," Randy said. "Don't chicken out on me, man. We've been through too much together. Besides, we can swim across that two hundred foot lake in a minute."

"Baloney," laughed Mike.

"Okay, maybe a little longer," Randy said, smiling. "Let's go. We'll only stay for a few minutes and swim back. Our clothes and food are already wrapped in plastic and we got plenty of water. Take everything else out of our packs and leave it here. Let's go."

"I don't like it," Mike said.

The two men were in the water and swimming furiously. The idea was to get out of the water as quickly as possible in order to minimize their exposure in case the debris dam gave way. They quickly reached the other side. Mike was thankful to be out of the water. It was too scary for him. Maybe I'm getting old, he thought. I am interested in staying alive however. That isn't getting old, just sensible. He shook his head, wondering why he let Randy talk him into this insane adventure.

"Wow!" Randy exclaimed, as he looked into the canyon in front of them.

From the trail side of the gorge from which they had always looked across to the side they were now on, all they could see was a semicircular hole in the gorge's east wall. There were trees and other greenery, but the rest of the view was blocked by the canyon walls. They imagined it to be only a shallow depression in the canyon wall, but always figured it a likely spot where Indians might have built small structures for living or storing grain. But, what they were now seeing shocked them.

The opening in the rocks was not a shallow depression, but a lush canyon extending for several miles. There must be plenty of water to support the abundant green trees and plants, they figured.

"We've got to explore this," Randy said.

"I have to agree with you," Mike replied. "It was a good idea I had, don't you think," he laughed. So did Randy. "You always have such good ideas, Mike."

Both men were still chuckling when they put on their dry clothes, slung their packs and canteens over their shoulders, and started into the beautiful canyon before them. Suddenly, they heard a thunderous crack behind them. They both realized the debris dam had burst and they instantly turned to look toward the lake.

The level of the lake was slowly but perceptibly dropping. A large whirlpool was spinning at the lake's north end, directly above the spot where the natural drainpipe carried water from the gorge. There was no way they could swim across the lake now. The current would carry them into the whirlpool and they would be sucked under the water. In minutes, the lake would be gone. They were trapped. The only way out was the canyon in front of them.

Mike shrugged. "We're committed now," he said. "Let's go."

The two men began walking into the lush canyon, awed by the incredible beauty. The red rock walls of this inner canyon contrasted with the deep green of the trees and bushes. After a quarter mile of hiking, they saw a fifty foot high waterfall which emptied into a clear, south flowing river.

"No problem with water," Randy said.

"I can't believe this canyon is so magnificent," Mike replied. "I've never seen anything so gorgeous."

"Hey, look over there," Randy exclaimed.

To their left was a vertical red wall. Must be about five hundred feet high," Mike said. "Look at the bottom area of the wall. It's covered with rock drawings, hundreds of petroglyphs.

"This place is fabulous!" Randy exclaimed, his self-satisfied tone underscoring the brilliance of his idea to come here. "Let's take a look," he shouted excitedly, as he began hustling toward the rock cliff. Mike followed along twenty feet behind him.

"Whoa," Mike suddenly yelled. "Did you hear that?"

"Believe it, buddy,' Randy answered excitedly. "I would have heard that rattle if I was standing on the other side of the canyon. That's gotta' be a heck of big rattlesnake to make that much noise."

"He's not close," Mike called back. "We're okay." But, Mike began thinking about what he just said. Generally speaking, a rattlesnake won't rattle unless a person or animal is close and threatening. The rattle is a warning, a sort of rule of engagement for the snake. "Come closer and I strike." Mike could tell from the sound of the rattle this snake was not close. But, the sound was loud, powerful. It wasn't the normal rattle or buzzing noise Mike had heard so many times before. This rattle seemed predatory, Mike thought, but that didn't make a lot of sense. He knew a rattlesnake will choose to retreat rather than risk injury or death in a fight. It will stay hidden if it's not bothered. It's not an aggressive snake like the water moccasin which will actually come after a person. But, this one......

Mike was jolted from his thoughts by Randy's yells from the base of the cliff. "Mike, you gotta' see this."

As he walked up to the spiraling red rock wall, he could see what Randy was so worked up about. The petroglyphs were unlike any either of the men had ever seen. Crisp, precisely drawn images of warriors with shields, animals and hovering, black spectral figures were artistically arranged in one area, while an adjacent section displayed fantastical monsters chasing and devouring villagers. There were huge snakes, mountain lions, bears and every manner of gigantic animal. The drawings were eerily realistic, seeming more like photographic snapshots than one thousand year old paintings.

"Mike, these drawings are incredible. I don't think anyone's ever been here before us."

"Except the people who drew them a thousand years ago," Mike reminded Randy.

Randy chuckled. "Yeah, you got a point there."

The men continued admiring the drawings and snapping pictures with their cell phones. As Mike took his photos, however, he was increasingly wondering about the motive for the ancients to draw over-size animals preying on people. Possibly there was some religious aspect to it, he guessed.

Although it was only three-thirty, the sun was moving lower toward the canyon's west wall. Afternoon shadows would soon spread across the canyon and create an artificial early dusk. "Do you want to travel further south in the canyon or spend the night here?" Mike asked.

"We ought to stay here tonight," Randy answered. "That will give us more time to explore the area and see what else we can find. Besides," he added, "there are still dark clouds floatin' around up there. We should try to find a cave in case it rains again. There's no use being caught out in the open if there's a thunderstorm. A nice dry cave would be comfy," he laughed.

"I agree," Mike replied. "But, we have to get serious about finding a way out of here tomorrow. If we can't find a trail to the top of the cliffs, we got troubles."

"Don't worry so much, Mike. The walls at the south end of the canyon don't look too bad, at least from here. We can hike there in an hour and find a nice little trail up the cliff. Trust me," he said.

"You're asking a lot," Mike laughed.

As the two men looked around, Mike spotted a large cave approximately seventy-five feet above the canyon floor. A natural trail up the east wall provided convenient access.

"This is too easy," Randy said. "I'm sure glad we decided to come here," he laughed.

"Alright, alright," Mike replied. "I admit it. I was wrong. It was a good idea to risk our lives and swim across the lake so we could see this place," he replied begrudgingly.

"Let's go check the cave out for rattlesnakes," Randy said. "It looks like the perfect place for them." The two men began moving up the cliff wall, and in a few minutes, reached the large opening of the chamber.

As they peered into the cavern, they could see it extended well over one hundred feet inward. Because of the angle of the sun, there was dim but adequate light from the cave's opening through the first fifty feet. Though the back part of the cavern had considerably less light, it was not totally dark. They had brought their flashlights for just such this situation. "You go ahead and check it out, Randy," Mike said. "I don't like snakes."

"No, I'm the one that doesn't like snakes," Randy grumbled. "There's probably mountain lions and bears in here too." He pulled out his flashlight and went into the cave.

He walked a few steps in and stopped to pick up a few small rocks. He threw one toward the back of the cave, figuring an animal in the darkness would respond with a warning rattle, or growl, in the worst case scenario. There was no sound and he threw the other rock. There was still no sound. He moved further into the cave, his flashlight pointed toward the darkness.

The cave was approximately fifty feet wide and twenty-five high. It was roomy, but spooky. He had just moved into the cavern's darker back section when his flashlight's circular beam flashed upon an astounding sight. "Jeez!" he exclaimed loudly.

"What is it, Randy?" Mike yelled.

"Get in here fast, man," he screamed. "You're never gonna' believe this."

Mike ran into the cave and was at Randy's side in seconds. "Unbelievable," he gasped, as the two men gazed at the huge skeleton. Whatever animal the bones belonged to had been huge. The rib section of the monster in front of them was as wide as they were tall, at least six feet. The skeleton extended further back into the cave. Though it was obvious the bones were ancient, both men wondered if its descendants were still around. Mike momentarily recalled the rattle they heard earlier. No way, he thought.

As the men followed the long column of bones further into the cave, it became obvious they were walking next to the skeleton of a gargantuan prehistoric snake. "It's at least fifty feet long," Randy said, as the row of bones veered away from the men.

"That must be where the head is," Mike replied. The snake's bones lay close to the cave's wall, forcing both men to squeeze past in order to get to the front portion of the creature. When they finally reached its head, they stood gazing in amazement. The hollow cavity of the snake's right eye was the same height as their eyes. They were standing eye to eye with a snake never seen by modern man. They snapped photos with their cell phones and squeezed back out of the tight area. "Rest in peace, brother," Randy said.

"This place is spooking me out," Randy said, his tone signaling he was serious.

"Yeah, it's not a real cozy place," Mike agreed. "We still have plenty of daylight left. Let's see if we can hike out of here."

"Fine with me," Randy replied, as the two men began to walk toward the front of the cave.

As they walked past the end of the gigantic snake skeleton, both men were relieved to see daylight and the cave entrance. What they didn't like however, was gray sky which had now become visible. "Looks like those clouds we saw earlier meant business," Mike said.

"Yeah," Randy answered reluctantly.

As they stood at the cave's entrance looking across the canyon, they could see the rain falling at the south wall. It wasn't a thunderstorm, but it was a heavy enough rain to convince them to make camp and stay in the cave overnight.

"We have plenty of food and water," Mike smiled. "We can sleep on those ledges so we'll be out of reach in case any garden variety rattlesnakes happen to wander in during the night."

"I guess it won't be so bad," Randy said.

They dropped their backpacks and scurried down the path to the canyon floor. They would get some firewood to discourage any curious large predators from paying them a visit after dark. To devise beds, they made several trips down the path, pulling branches from pine trees and retrieving handfuls of dry, brown pine needles lying on the ground.

They had just completed their final trip back up the trail to the cave when the rain started. They constructed their beds on the rock shelves ten feet above the cave floor and built a fire. It was time to relax, and they munched on the snacks they'd brought and looked out at the rain until darkness came. Randy threw a few more pieces of wood on the fire and the men walked over to the cave wall and climbed up to turn in.

"Hey these pine branch beds are pretty nice," Randy said.

Mike laughed. "They aren't that nice, but they're better than lying directly on the cold rocks. Goodnight," he said.

It was several hours later when the thunder began, loud rumbles ricocheting off the cave's walls and explosive lightning streaks igniting the sky. Randy was the first to wake, but Mike was a close second. "Who started the war?" Mike gasped.

The storm lasted nearly an hour, and as it faded, so did Randy and Mike. Once again, they were asleep.

It was perhaps two hours later when both men were awakened by the sound of movement. The storm had passed, replaced by a bright moon which provided a degree of illumination at the front of the cave where they lay. As they looked into the darkness at the back of the cave, they could see nothing. The strange noise continued, heavy but stealthy, as if something large was being dragged toward them.

Suddenly they saw it and were overwhelmed by terror. A massive snake was slowly moving past them, its enormous head just a foot below where they lay frozen with fear. The snake stopped for a moment to look around, its tongue darting from its mouth to sense possible prey or predators in the vicinity. Randy and Mike were thinking they might become dinner, but the snake moved on, his immense body taking what seemed like years to pass by and leave the cave.

"That snake is as big as the skeleton we saw at the back of the cave," Randy whispered in a shaking voice.

"You're telling me," Mike agreed. "We gotta' get out of here before that guy comes back."

They jumped up from their makeshift beds, looked toward the cave entrance to make sure the snake wasn't coming back, and slid down the rock wall to the floor of the cave.

"Stay here, Randy," Mike said. "I'll go check outside the cave to make sure our friend's gone.

"No argument there,' Randy agreed. As Mike crept toward the cave entrance, Randy shined his flashlight toward the rear of the cavern. He had been able to see the massive snake skeleton from this spot when they first came upon the cave. But, now it was gone. Randy took several more steps further into the cave. He could now see the back of the cave. The snake's skeleton was gone.

"Randy!" Mike whispered excitedly. "Where the heck are you?"

"Back here," Randy replied. Mike quickly walked toward him.

"Are you nuts?" Mike said, careful to not raise his voice.

"Mike," Randy answered, "the skeleton is gone."

"What?" Mike said, as he strained his eyes to see into the darkness. He grabbed Randy's light and quickly shined it around the rear of the cave. Randy was right. The snake's skeleton was not there.

"Come on, let's get out of here now," Mike said. "Move it."

The men kept low as the crept out of the cave's entrance. With the bright moonlight, they could see nearly all the way to the south end of the canyon. Nothing was visible but the rocks, trees and river. However, they decided to move to higher ground and wait for daylight before they started their walk to the south end of the canyon. They climbed another one hundred feet up the canyon wall to wait for the dawn. The snake couldn't reach them here. There was no trail it could follow and the monster couldn't climb sheer canyon walls.

Mike and Randy never really slept. They watched the cave's entrance far below them, waiting for the snake to return. But, it never did. "You know this place is haunted," Mike said.

Randy shook his head. "Let's just get out of here as soon as we can," he answered.

The dawn came. They didn't want to start their hike with the monster lurking somewhere out there in the relatively small area of the canyon, but they had no choice. It was several hours later when the two men reached the top of the south wall. They looked back into the canyon behind them. Their hike had been uneventful and they were thankful they were still alive. "We're safe now," Mike said.

They began walking south, figuring they would eventually come across a trail or people.

They had walked half a mile when they saw the petroglyphs on the side of the high cliff. The men recoiled as they gazed at the drawings of oversize snakes, mountain lions and bears eating warriors with shields and chasing villagers. They heard thunder and looked up to see dark clouds. A storm was coming.

Cowboy Hell

"It's real simple, Bubba," the big bull bluntly stated. "You get treated the same way down here in Hell the way you treated us cows up on earth. Is that so hard for you to understand?"

"Excuse me, sir," the distressed cowboy interrupted, but my name ain't Bubba. It's Conrad Hilson, just like the hotel except I got a "s" where they got a "t."

Conrad Hilson would never have been so respectful to any animal. "Animals was animals," he always said. At one time or other in Conrad Hilson's life, he had come across every type of creature known to God and man, and some which wasn't. He never had a whole lot of regard for any of them. But, this bull was different. He was a figure of considerable authority down here in Hell. Conrad still wasn't clear on how he happened to end up here and that was the nature of his inquiry.

"The fact of the matter is this, Conrad," the bull continued. "You happened to have dropped dead exactly two hours, thirty-seven minutes, and let me check," pausing looking at his watch, "eighteen seconds ago. You're mine now, Conrad. I'm in control.

You better be appreciative that I'm taking time out of my busy schedule to explain things to your sorry personage, not that I owe you that courtesy after treating us animals up there the way you did," he said pointing upward with his right hoof. "Most deceased people go to heaven or 'straight to hell,' as the saying goes," but, not cowboys."

"Well, that's not quite the case," he added, contradicting himself. "Good cowboys do go to heaven, but bad cowboys go to a special kind of place appropriately designated, 'Cowboy Hell.' And here you are."

"Danged if I ain't," Conrad reluctantly agreed. "I'm findin' this to be a might uncomfortable discussion, if you don't mind my sayin' so."

"You can say anything your little heart desires, Conrad," the big bull responded. "Fact of the matter is, nobody down here's gonna' pay any attention to you anyway."

"So you're the head man, bull, I mean," Conrad said. "How'd they happen to choose you?"

"That's a long story but I don't have the time or interest to relate it to the likes of you," the bull answered.

"Well, could you give me maybe just a hint?" Conrad asked.

"You think that knowing about me is gonna' help get you outta' here?" the bull asked.

"Well I was hopin' I could somehow work my way into your good graces and get out of this place possibly. I was just thinkin' about that, don't you know?"

"What the hell, and that's so appropriate an expression in this particular place, do you mean by 'don't you know?' And, do you think this place is some kind of monopoly game and you can pass and go or something?"

"Well I just wanted to know how you came to have your particular job," Conrad countered, "and how I might make amends for my badly lived life."

"Alright, I'll tell you, Conrad," the big bull agreed. "I got to be head man down here, dang, now you got me talking like you, the head bull, I mean, because up on earth, my name was Devil Bull. I was as mean as you, Conrad. Of course, I had reason to be. They put a flank strap on me to get me to buck at the rodeos, and when I wanted to be friendly, they zapped me with five thousand volts of electricity with their 'Hot-Shot' device. Dang, that stung.

Anyway, after ten years of performing under not the best of working conditions, I got fed up one day and flipped some cowboy like you into the stands and he landed on his head, probably his least vulnerable spot since he didn't have any brains anyway. He ended up dead either way and they decided I was too mean and they killed me too. They figured I broke so many cowboy bones and delivered so much pain, my kinda' days were over. That's how I got here and came to be in charge of Cowboy Hell. I'd say I've come up in the world, if we weren't so far down in Hell, don't you know. Dang, your colloquialisms are infectious, Conrad."

Conrad knew he was in trouble. He had roped, castrated and branded thousands of cows. Oh yeah, he stapled plastic labels on their ears too. All that must have caused great annoyance and displeasure for those beasts, though Conrad had never given it any thought because he was the deliverer, not the receiver of the pain. What the hell, he always thought, what do they expect, egg in their beer? But, suddenly, there was the sound of hope, of escape from Cowboy Hell.

"You can get out of Cowboy Hell, Conrad, but there's only one way," Devil Bull said.

"And what would that way be?" Conrad asked.

"You have to win a little game we play down here," Devil Bull replied. "The rules are a little regimented and disagreeable, sort of like Republicans."

"What game is that?" Conrad asked.

"It's called 'Balls of Fire.' That's so fitting, this being Hell and all, don't you know. Dang, now you got me where I can't stop sayin' that, Conrad."

"Sorry about that," Conrad said. "How does your game work? Somethin' tells me I ain't gonna' like it, don't you know."

"Stop sayin' that stupid 'don't you know' phrase, Conrad. You're drivin' me nuts. Alright, listen up. Here's the rules. We have a castration machine, an exact duplicate of what you used on us cows. You know, it's like a paper shredder machine, except with a slightly bigger opening to accommodate testicles. Didn't you used to call it the 'welcome wagon' because when the machine chopped the cows' balls off, they would drop into it?"

"Yeah, we did call it the welcome wagon," Conrad agreed. "And, the place we inserted their testicles into the top of the machine was called the 'in-box.'"

"Anyway, what you have to do is strip naked and position yourself on the castration machine and insert your testicles into the 'in-box.'"

"Easy enough," Conrad said. "Of course, I don't want to get them chopped off or nothin' like that."

"Of course you don't, Conrad. What would be the point of that?"

"Then what happens?" Conrad asked.

"Well, one of us cows stands behind you and holds a lighted match by your rear end so you can pass gas and induce a small explosion. It's nothin' huge, of course, like the Feds would come and investigate, or anything like that. It's just a pleasant little detonation that will give us Hell management cows a chuckle."

"Yeah, I've seen guys do that before," Conrad agreed. "I've never done it myself, but it is definitely possible to accomplish. So, all I gotta' is fart and I'm outta' here."

"Not exactly. Remember I said there are rules, which brings us to the point of why your testicles are in the in-box of the castration machine, aka welcome wagon."

"And they would be?" Conrad inquired.

"You see, Conrad, once you are positioned on the castration machine, you have exactly five seconds to accomplish your gaseous feat."

"Oh," said Conrad apprehensively. "And what happens if I don't manage to break wind in the five second limit?"

"The welcome wagon timer is set for five seconds. If you can't achieve ignition, as they say at NASA, in that five seconds the welcome wagon activates and castrates you. Pretty straight forward, wouldn't you say?"

"Yeah, I suppose," Conrad reluctantly agreed. "But, I'm willing to give it a try if it will get me out of Cowboy Hell."

"Oh, it will, Conrad, but there is one more rule," Devil Bull said.

"Yeah," Conrad said, fearing the worst.

"Yeah," Devil Bull said. "You have to produce twenty blasts within twelve minutes. Think you can do that?"

"That ain't fair," Conrad protested.

"Of course it's not," Devil Bull agreed. "But, this is Cowboy Hell. What do you expect? And the good thing is when you get castrated, and you will, your testicles grow back so you can get castrated again. You can get castrated over and over, and other than hurting like hell, no pun intended, no harm done. And, our team is always there to offer encouragement and cheer you onward and upward, being that's the direction heaven is in."

All of that happened eleven years ago. In that period of time, Conrad has been castrated 1476 times. The good thing is he has reached a plateau of thirteen flammable farts in a row. That is truly admirable. And, if Conrad continues working as hard as he has, he will earn his way out of Cowboy Hell in exactly four years and three months, give or take.

(Adapted from the novel *Invasion of the Moon Women* by James Wharton.)

HOMUNCULI

Gremlins

The B-26 Martin Marauder was in a fatal high-speed dive, losing altitude fast. If Mary Jane Kicheloe couldn't pull the twin engine bomber back to level flight, the three women on board would be dead in less than a minute.

What had started out as a routine flight from the Martin factory at Middle River, Maryland had abruptly become a fight for survival high over Page, Arizona. Mary Jane and her crew were WASP's, Women Airforce Service Pilots recruited in World War Two to transport airplanes.

The B-26 normally carried a crew of seven in combat however it only required a team of three to ferry the airplane across the country. Besides Mary Jane, there was a co-pilot and a navigator/radio operator. It was early 1943 and their job was to fly airplanes from the factory to military airfields.

The B-26 was difficult to fly and inexperienced pilots had a high accident rate. Although Mary Jane was one of the best WASP pilots, strange, unexplainable things were happening on this flight. She had no idea how to handle them. They were headed to Long Beach Army Airfield and their present position was fifty miles northeast of Page, Arizona. They were flying at 18,000 feet. That's when the trouble started.

Navigator/radio operator Billie Jacoby saw a misty shape float through the bomb bay area. She moved to the cockpit to ask pilot Mary Jane about the phenomenon. Both women dismissed the mist as not important. As they talked however, the bomb bay doors began opening and closing wildly. Billie went back to take a look. She quickly did a manual override and the bomb bay doors slammed shut. Billie wondered if the mist she saw had anything to do with the bomb bay doors going crazy.

Then the airplane started "wagging," that is, the tail of the airplane began swinging from side to side. Mary Jane pushed hard on opposite rudders but couldn't get the big bomber under control.

"Billie," she yelled, "go back there and see what's going on."

Billie quickly moved toward the rear of the plane and stuck her head into the dorsal turret, which was normally manned by a gunner with two machine guns. She looked back at the tail and was horrified.

"Mary Jane," she called, "there are two little men playing seesaw on the tail, pushing it from side to side."

"What?" Mary Jane barked into the intercom. "You have your oxygen mask on, Billie?"

"Mary Jane," she screamed, "they are out there on the tail trying to crash the plane! There are two little men with beards and stocking hats dressed in red and green outfits and wearing black boots. They can't be more than two feet tall. And they're laughing. They know they're scaring us to death."

"Joan," Mary Jane shouted to her co-pilot, "get back there and see what's wrong with Billie. She's hallucinating."

Joan unhooked her seat belt and quickly moved toward the rear of the plane. Billie was still looking out the dorsal turret window toward the tail of the aircraft.

"Get out of there and let me take a look, Billie!" Joan yelled excitedly.

The engine noise made it difficult for the women to hear and the tail swinging from side to side made it hard to keep their balance. As Joan stuck her head into the dorsal turret, she couldn't believe her eyes. It was just as Billie reported. There were two little men with beards literally pushing the tail toward one another causing dangerous control problems for the pilot. And, just as she had also said, the little men were laughing.

"Mary Jane," Joan called into the intercom, "we've got gremlins on board. There are two on our tail and that misty shape Billie saw must also have been one. We've got to land the plane immediately."

Mary Jane had heard reports from the combat areas about gremlins on airplanes. The mischievous little men misaligned bomb sights, caused engines to fail, and made instruments go haywire. She thought that the term "gremlins" was a catch-all kind of term for imaginary wee people pilots blamed for unexplained problems. She never thought they were real. However, she did recall that some pilots swore they actually saw gremlins and described them exactly as Billie and Joan had.

"Good Lord," she said, they are real."

"Mary Jane," Joan called from the dorsal turret, "traffic at three o'clock."

Mary Jane had already seen the four fighter planes which were probably based in Phoenix and on a training mission. They were flying east in tight formation. Suddenly, however, the right wingman peeled his airplane off from the group and headed straight for the B-26.

"What is he doing?" Mary Jane yelled to Joan. "He's coming straight at us."

"Why doesn't he turn?" Joan screamed back, as she climbed back into her seat on the right side of the cockpit.

"He's got to see us," Mary Jane shouted, "but he just keeps coming."

"Hold on, Billie!" Mary Jane yelled into the intercom. "We're going into a hard dive."

But the fighter plane was diving too, still coming right at them. The gremlins were intent on bringing the B-26 down and were somehow causing the fighter plane to steer right at their bomber so it would crash into them.

"There must be gremlins aboard the fighter too!" Mary Jane exclaimed. "Pull up, you idiot!" she screamed into the mike, hoping the fighter pilot was on the same radio frequency. "He can't control his airplane either! Pull up!" she shrieked again.

But it was to no avail because the gremlins were calling the shots. Mary Jane saw the fighter pilot bail out just before his plane crashed into the right side of the B-26 fuselage, leaving a gaping hole which ran diagonally from top to bottom on the airplane's right side. Apparently only the fighter plane's wing hit their B-26. However, Mary Jane was now struggling to bring the big bomber out of the dive.

"Pull hard, Joan!" she screamed. "Pull hard with everything you've got!"

Both pilots had their yokes pulled back all the way but the plane wouldn't level off. It was diving directly toward the town of Page, Arizona. Not only would the three women in the crew die, but many people on the ground would also be killed.

Mary Jane and Joan looked at each other. The engines were screaming and air was roaring through the huge hole in the right side of the plane. The town of Page was coming at them fast. If they didn't pull the plane out of the dive in the next critical seconds, they would crash into the small city. But the two pilots couldn't pull the plane to a level flight attitude.

"This is it!" Mary Jane screamed. "We're going in!"

"No!" screamed Joan. "I don't want to die!"

"Do something, Mary Jane!" Billie screamed into her ear.

The town was so close they could actually see people walking around. They would crash into the town in a few seconds and a lot of people would die.

Suddenly, the nose of the airplane responded to the two women who were still pulling hard on their yokes. As the nose of the airplane began to rise toward the horizon, the "G" forces pinned the women to their seats. The engines were on full power and roared loudly as the airplane strained hard to stop losing altitude. Then the "G" force decreased to normal as the plane reached the level-off point. The plane was flying over two hundred miles per hour and was no more than forty feet above the ground.

"Look out!" Mary Jane screamed as the plane roared past the town's water tower, missing it by inches.

The left wing clipped the top of a tall tree and Mary Jane pulled back slightly and the elevators shifted the plane into a gentle climb. They didn't climb far however. Joan pointed out the Page airport and Mary Jane banked the B-26 in a hard left turn and headed directly for the small air field. They landed the plane quickly and shut down the engines.

When they climbed out of the airplane, they were astonished at the damage the bomber had sustained. The tail was beaten up and had large dents in it. The left horizontal stabilizer was bent upward. And the gash in the right side of the airplane was so large, Mary Jane was surprised the airplane wasn't cut in half.

As the three women stood surveying their wrecked airplane, they heard voices and hysterical laughter. Under the tail section of the B-26 were three little bearded men dressed in red and green. They were pointing at the still very rattled women and laughing at them. Suddenly, they disappeared.

Note: In 1943, Allied Headquarters in North Africa set up Gremlin Detector Squads to deal with "gremlin events" as they were called. Gremlins were especially prevalent in the

North Africa Theater as well as Great Britain. Numerous air crew members reported actually seeing the "little people" described above.

From the short story collection *Ghosts of the Grand Canyon Country* by James Wharton.

Wardell

May the sun always shine upon you because if it doesn't,
someone has turned it around backwards.

There are all kinds of people. Unfortunately Ranger Randy wasn't one of them. He had been with the forest service for thirty-one years. They say he knew the forest so well he actually had conversations with it. This was a concern for his fellow rangers and the occasional tourist who would approach him to ask a question while he was talking to a pine tree.

At heart, Ranger Randy was a very nice fellow, always looking at the bright side of life. Once when he attended a colleague's funeral, he reminded the deceased man's wife that the first three letters in funeral spell fun.

Though he was always considered eccentric, his troubles didn't really begin until his Neanderthal man came along. He found the almost human creature packed in an ice floe during an early spring thaw. Ranger Randy hacked him out of the ice and brought him home to live with him. His wife of thirty years ago, as he referred to her, had moved out thirty years ago. Ranger Randy had lived alone all those years and decided he wanted company.

The Neanderthal, who was named Wardell, was just what the doctor ordered. (Though I have no formal medical training, I believe that I can say with confidence that it is doubtful any doctor would ever order a Neanderthal man to cure loneliness. However, if one ever did, this would be the situation which called for it.)

As with all Neanderthal men, there were several complications. First, no one could see Wardell but Ranger Randy. "Being invisible is just a part of who he is," Ranger Randy explained. "You see, he's also a very deceptive person. I never know whether to believe him or not. He lies so much, the mirror never knows if it's his real reflection."

Ranger Randy often complained to his co-workers about his Neanderthal friend Wardell. "He never pays for his coffee when we go to the café," Ranger Randy told them. "Wardell says the café uses re-poured coffee. That's coffee that's already been poured into customers' cups, but they didn't drink it all and left it on the table when they were finished eating. He says the café takes the used coffee and pours it back into the pot and then re-pours it into new customers' cups. But, I think the real reason Wardell won't pay is because, like all Neanderthals, he's short and he thinks no one will see him when he sneaks out without paying his bill. But, he's invisible. Nobody sees him anyway. He's perplexing."

Ranger Randy also maintains that some of the things Wardell says confuse him. "Just the other night I heard a noise in the hallway," he told me. "The next morning I asked Wardell if he was walking around the house last night. 'Yeah,' he said. 'I was. I heard a noise so I got up to check it out. As I walked down the hall, who should I run into but myself? I couldn't believe it was me, so I moved my arms up and down and made funny faces to see if I was looking in the mirror. I thought someone might have left a full length mirror in the hall. Anyway, I moved my arms up and down to see if I could keep up with myself, because mirror or not, I should be able to keep up with myself. And I couldn't. So I knew it wasn't me."

"One day I got a birthday card from Wardell," Ranger Randy continued. "It read as follows: 'Happy Birthday in advance this year in case I didn't remember last year's until now and next year's last year and didn't want to wait because I might the year after, in which case I did, and it would all be in vain. So I didn't."

'Besides,' the card continued, 'if the day and month stay the same, why should the year change? That would mean you were just born. Or, if the day and the month could change when the year changed, that would re-synchronize things very nicely, but no, that will never be. At least not this year. With love, Wardell.'

"We've got other issues," Ranger Randy added. "Many of the trees, rocks and plants in the forest are friends of mine. I truly love them. However, Wardell doesn't agree that someone can love inanimate objects. His philosophy is, 'If it don't poop, it ain't worth lovin."

"And Wardell is always making stupid jokes. He says things like, 'I'm not always right, but I'm right as often as I am left.' I don't get it. He told me an old Neanderthal proverb, which says, 'May the sun always shine upon you. Because, if it doesn't, someone has turned it around backwards." Then he gets a serious look on his face like what he said was so profound."

"And when he gets mad," Ranger Randy continued, "he curses a blue streak. I mean he says some awful words like I've never heard in the forest. Makes me blush."

"He's got a dog, or at least he used to have a dog 30,000 years ago when he lived in Europe. 'My dog's name was Ed,' he says. 'I called him Ed the wonder dog. He used to sit on the porch all day and wonder,' Wardell explained."

"That just shows to go you,' Wardell said. 'Ed sat there wondering and now, all these years later, here I am and Ed is long gone. I ain't ever wondered about nothing. I'm alive and Ed isn't. That's gotta' tell you something."

"I corrected Wardell on his 'shows to go you' quip. You mean that just goes to show you, don't you, Wardell?" I asked.

"No. I meant what I said," Wardell answered. "He obviously can't take criticism."

Anyway, the government psychiatrist Dr. Nesbitt Kirkelganger examined Ranger Randy to see if he was possibly losing it. His conclusion was "He's definitely doing things not on the menu. That pet Neanderthal he thinks he has is the biggest problem. People become frightened when they see Ranger Randy talking to an invisible Neanderthal man. On the whole however, Ranger Randy is fit for service. What we need to work on is to convince him there are no Neanderthals left on earth. They died off thirty thousand years ago."

It was decided that Dr. Nesbitt Kirkelganger should explain to Ranger Randy that Neanderthals no longer exist. They're all long dead. And that was exactly what he did.

Ranger Randy didn't argue. "I'm tired of Wardell anyway," he said. "I tried to teach him to drive and he took my car apart. It's in the garage now in about a thousand pieces. Neanderthals are very mechanically inclined. He did a real nice job of disassembling my car. He couldn't put it back together however. Anyway, he's gone now. He said something about greener pastures and I haven't seen him since."

Dr. Kirkelganger announced the good news. Things could get back to normal now. That evening when he arrived home, Dr. Kirkelganger had his usual two martinis, ate dinner and went to bed. He slept well, knowing he had cured Ranger Randy's imaginary friend problem.

After breakfast the next morning, Dr. Kirkelganger poured a cup of coffee to drink while he drove to work. He walked down the hallway and went through the door and into his garage. "Oh good lord," his wife heard him scream. "Marian," he called frantically.

As Marian pulled open the door to the garage, she too was shocked. Carefully laid out on the floor of the garage were at least one thousand parts that used to be Dr. Kirkelganger's Mercedes.

Only one word was painted on the wall. "Wardell"

Alma

"Eyahhhh!" came a shriek directly above me as the tree's branches cracked and shattered. I quickly ratiocinated something large was crashing through them, but before I could figure out what ratiocinated meant, a large, apelike creature crashed on the ground before me. "Dang," it yelled, "I keep forgetting I don't have a tail."

To say I was startled would be an understatement. So I won't say it. However, I was astonished, which means the same thing. And it scared the bejeebers out of me to boot. As I looked at the hair covered creature, it seemed as upset as I was about the situation, although it didn't exactly say so.

"I do that all the time," the creature said, getting to its feet. "Back in the old days, we used to have tails. Don't have 'em no more however. The problem is, when I want to hang down from a branch, my brain tells me my non-existent tail is holding on. Of course, it can't be, but since my brain is about a sixth the size of human brains, I ain't smart enough to remember my brain's fooling me and there's no tail back there. So, I fall out of trees over and over and over. Ouch. That smarts. Oh, and I'm Alma, by the way."

The thing was a little over four feet tall and I was no longer fearful. The fact that it could talk seemed unusual, but not frightening. "I'm Sydney. What are you?" I asked.

"I'm an Australopithecus," she answered. "I'm a ghost and I've been dead for a while. I lived 1.9 million years ago. I have no idea how I got here. I went to sleep in a tree one night and I woke up in a different place and time. That's weird, huh. Come to think of it, you look a little weird yourself, buddy. How old are you?"

"I'm seventy-four," I replied. "I live here at Shady Acres Senior Community."

"Oh," she replied, unimpressed. "Look, I need a place to stay until I figure out my life and how to get back to where I came from. Could I stay here with you for a while?"

I pondered that possibility, but not for long. "They don't allow pets," I said. "Sorry, you're out of luck."

"Pet!" the little apelike thing exclaimed. "I'm your great grand-mother several hundred thousand times removed. If anything, you're my pet."

I didn't like the little monster. She looked like an ogre out of a child's story book. "Well, just the same," I said. "You can't stay with me. There's only one bed in my room."

"I don't mind sleeping with you," she said, as long as you keep your hands to yourself. It's not that we Australopithecus types have higher moral standards than you humans, I'm just not at all attracted to you."

"You're nothing to write home about yourself," I countered.

She grunted, flippantly dismissing my cutting sarcasm. Although she was only four feet tall, had a misshapen face and was covered with black hair, the way she grunted and tossed aside my comment was kind of sexy. I suddenly felt attracted to the gruesome little creature.

"Look, I'll let you stay the night," I said. "You go around to the back of the building and knock on the sixth window. That's my room and I'll let you in. Wait a few minutes so I have time to find you some clothes."

"Okay," she said, and trotted off into the bushes. She looked better from the back than the front, I thought. Hmnn.

I went directly back into the building and headed to Mrs. Mathieson's room. "Mrs. Mathieson, I need to borrow a dress, some nice shoes and a nightgown. Can you help me out?"

"Sure Sydney," she said. She pulled a dress and pair of shoes from her closet and took a nightgown from the drawer. "You'll look nice in these, Sydney. I hope the shoes aren't too tight. I always thought you were a little swishy."

"Those things aren't for me, Mrs. Mathieson," I replied defensively.

"Oh, I know that, Sydney," she said, giving me a knowing wink. "Don't worry dear. It will be our little secret," she giggled.

"No really," I protested.

"Here, take your clothes and run along, Sydney," she said, shaking her head knowingly.

I left Mrs. Mathieson's room with the clothes. As I walked into my room, I saw Alma leering in my window and waving. I quickly shut the door to my room and walked over to open the window for her.

"What took you so long?" she asked.

"I had to find something for you to wear," I answered. "You've got to pretend you're civilized and put on this dress and shoes. I had to help Alma with the dress. She'd never worn one. Although the shoes barely fit, she somehow got into them. They were also a novelty and she seemed particularly taken with them.

"Now look," I said, "we're going to go down to the dining room for dinner. You just do exactly as I do. I'll tell the staff you're a guest. Okay."

"Yes, of course, Sydney," Alma replied, as she followed me out the door.

We were soon seated at my customary table. Normally four of us men sat there but tonight, one of the seats was vacant. Bill Naumsley was in the hospital having an operation.

"Who's your friend, Sydney?" Normie asked.

"This is Alma. She's an old friend of mine," I replied. Alma, this is Normie and the quiet fellow over there is Hargood."

Normie leaned over to whisper in my ear. "She's a real looker, Sydney, but tell her to shave her legs."

"Okay, Normie," I replied. How he happened to notice the black hair covering her legs but completely miss the equally generous covering of hair on her face and arms mystified me.

"Sydney, it's dance night after dinner. You think I might have a dance or two with Alma?"

"Ask Alma," I said.

"What do you say, Alma?" Normie asked. "Will you dance with me later?"

"Yes, Normie," Alma answered, smiling brightly. I had noticed her watching Normie earlier. She agreed to dance with him without even thinking about it. I felt the jealousy welling up inside me.

"Alma, they have to clear the tables and let the band get set up. If Sydney wouldn't mind, perhaps you would accompany me to my room and I could show you my etchings. I'm very good at them, you know."

"I'd love to see them, Normie," Alma quickly agreed.

"We'll be back in a few minutes, Sydney," Normie said, as he and Alma left the table and walked hand in hand out of the dining room.

"You ain't ever gonna' see that dame again," Hargood said, breaking his self-imposed code of silence.

Fifteen minutes passed. Then half an hour had gone by. The band had started to play and there was no sign of Alma or Normie. Hargood suggested we go to Normie's room to investigate. When we got there, the door was shut, but I quickly pushed it open, intent on saving my girl-friend from the lecherous Normie.

Hargood and I were astonished. There was no one in the room and Normie's window was open. We reported them missing. A search was immediately launched, but sadly, neither of them was ever found.

I think about them now and them. All I could figure out was that Alma must have found a way to get back to her own time of 1.9 million years ago. She must have brought Normie with her. He must be eighty years old, I thought. Imagine Alma getting hooked up with an old goat like that. I was only seventy-four. How could she choose that old codger over me?

Maybe she wasn't good with numbers. She did say her brain was only one-sixth the size of a human brain. That must be it.

HARUM-SCARUM

Lester Haney De-parted

It is written that one must look before one can see.
Yet, there are those who can see, but never look.
They are known as potheads.

Dr. Petra Auguerre stared at the grizzled cowboy sitting in her patient counselling room. He must be about forty-five she thought, although he looked to be about seventy-five. She decided to ask. "So, how old are you, Mr. Haney?"

"I'm forty-five, ma'am," he replied. "I don't look a day over thirty, do I," he said proudly.

"You don't look like you're even thirty," Dr. Auguerre, said. At least it was an honest answer, she thought. "What exactly is the problem you're experiencing, Mr. Haney?" she asked. "Nurse Thrush said you were having nightmares, I believe."

"Call me, Lester," he replied. "All my friends call me, Lester."

"Alright, Lester," Dr. Auguerre agreed, though not really wanting to be included in Lester Haney's list of friends.

"Is Nurse Thrush's name, Thrush?" Lester asked.

"Yes, it is, Lester. Why do you ask?"

"Thrush is a bird, ain't it?"

"Yes, that's right, Lester," she answered. "A thrush is a songbird in the family Turdidae. It has brownish upper plumage and a spotted breast." Dr. Auguerre prided herself on knowing every detail about her employees. Dr. Auguerre also liked to use her marvelous comic wit to put her patients at ease so she often made funny jokes. "Of course, our Nurse Thrush doesn't have brownish upper plumage and a spotted breast," she said, thinking her patient would burst out laughing at her clever quip.

"Oh," Lester Haney said, apparently thinking Nurse Thrush not having brownish upper plumage and a spotted breast was a good thing.

"Let's get back to your problem, Lester," Dr. Auguerre said, wishing to quickly move on.

"It ain't nightmares, ma'am. I told Nurse what's her name it warn't nightmares. It's real things happenin' to me."

"Her name is Nurse Thrush," the doctor replied. "What kinds of things are happening to you, Lester?"

"Well, look at this," he said, pulling off his left cowboy boot and sock.

Dr. Auguerre noticed Lester Haney was missing three toes, but other than that, his left foot appeared to be normal. And smelly. "I don't see anything wrong with your foot, Lester," she said.

"What!" Lester exclaimed. "You don't see that I'm missin' three toes?"

"Of course I see you're missing three toes, Lester, but you're foot is fine."

"Do you not understand I'm here because I'm missing three toes?" he asked in exasperation.

"Lester," Dr. Auguerre replied impatiently, your three largest toes have obviously been missing for some time. Did you have some sort of accident and have them removed?"

"No, Dr. Auguerre," Lester answered in frustration. "When I went to bed last night, all my toes were on my foot. I wake up this morning, and three toes are gone, vanished."

Dr. Auguerre leaned forward and took hold of Lester's left foot. She looked at it closely. "Lester, there is no damage to the area your toes once occupied. They have obviously been missing for quite some time."

"No, they were on my foot last night, Doctor." Someone stole them while I slept. I want my toes back."

Dr. Auguerre was becoming frustrated herself. There was obviously nothing wrong with this man's foot. The toes had to have been removed by a skilled surgeon years ago. There weren't even any scars where he amputated.

"Lester," Dr. Auguerre said," I'm very busy. There's nothing wrong with your left foot other than the missing toes which were removed long ago. Think back. You must have had an accident and the toes had to be amputated."

"Doctor, do you think I'm some kind of idiot?" Lester replied. "I'm telling you my left foot had all five toes last night and there were three missing when I got out of bed this morning."

Actually, Dr. Aguerre did think Lester Haney was some kind of idiot. Or else he was crazy. Since she held an advanced degree in psychiatry, Dr. Auguerre decided to handle Lester's case as a mental issue. The money was also much better with a psychiatric diagnosis and work-up.

"Alright, Lester," she humored him, "so you went to bed with ten toes and woke up with only seven. Is that correct?"

"Yeah, Doc, exactly," an obviously relieved Lester replied.

"How did you feel about that?" she asked.

"How would you feel if you woke up and found that three toes on your left foot were missing?" Lester replied.

"I'll ask the questions," Dr. Auguerre replied, jealously guarding that professional boundary separating the questioner from the questionee. "So, how did you feel about that?"

"I felt the same way I did when I woke up last week with my right foot missing," Lester Haney replied.

"What!" Dr. Auguerre exclaimed.

"I said, I felt..." Dr. Auguerre interrupted Lester Haney's answer. "You lost your right foot last week?" she asked.

"Yes, that's what I've been trying to tell you people. I'm losing body parts. Every couple days I wake up and something's gone. See," he said, raising his left hand, "two fingers missing. That happened ten days ago."

Dr. Auguerre decided that hypnosis was the best way to approach Lester Haney's problem. She would have to do a reversion analysis whereby she would hypnotize Lester Haney and bring him back to where he was when he lost two fingers from his left hand ten days ago. It wasn't difficult to hypnotize Lester Haney. He was a simple man. A very simple man, actually.

"You are sleeping, Lester. You are in your bed ten days ago. What is happening?"

"I'm snoring," he said.

"Besides that," Dr. Auguerre said impatiently. "What else is happening in your room?"

"There's a raccoon in my bed," Lester yelled loudly. Nurse Thrush rushed into the counseling room. "My god, Dr. Auguerre," she screamed. "Is everything alright?"

"Yes, Nurse Thrush," she said. "Now get out," she added brusquely.

"Alright," Lester Haney said, and stood up.

"No, not you, Lester."

"Okay," Lester said, and he sat back down.

"What's the raccoon doing?" Dr. Auguerre asked.

"He's bitin' off two fingers from my left hand," Lester screamed. "Ouch. That hurt!"

"Alright, Lester," Dr. Auguerre continued, "let's go back to last week when you lost your right foot. What happened then?"

Lester thought for a minute. "I'm asleep in my bed, again," he said. "There's a coyote in bed with me!" Lester exclaimed.

"What's he doing, Lester?" Dr. Auguerre asked.

"He's biting off my right foot," Lester replied. "Whoa, that don't feel too swell," he said. "Ow!"

"Alright, Lester, what happened this week when you lost the three toes on your left foot?"

Lester paused to reflect on Dr. Auguerre's question. "I'm asleep in my bed again. I see him now. A snapping turtle is in bed with me. He's a big one too. He's chomping off the three toes on my left foot."

"Why do you think these animals are doing this, Lester?" Dr. Auguerre asked.

"It's simple, doc," he said. "I see it all now. They're takin' revenge on me."

"These are all animals I've shot or killed earlier in my life, doc. They're all dead now but they're hauntin' me, payin' me back for what I done to 'em when they was alive. Oh my lord, what am I gonna' do?" a distressed Lester Haney wailed.

Again, Nurse Thrush burst through the office door. "Is everything alright, Dr. Auguerre?" she cried, a frantic expression on her face.

"Get out!" Dr. Auguerre screamed.

"Alright, Dr. Auguerre," Lester Haney said, standing up.

"No, not you, Lester," she said, reaching the limit of her frustration.

"Oh," Lester said, and he sat back down.

*

"It was the strangest case I've ever seen," Dr. Auguerre said to Dr. Kromley, as they stood looking into the empty coffin at Lester Haney's wake." It was apparently an extreme psychosomatic response to a severe guilt complex. You see, Lester Haney had killed many animals during his lifetime. He obviously felt very guilty about it and his brain compensated for this guilt by creating the illusion that these animals had come back as ghosts and were paying Lester back for his cruelty by eating parts of his body. This illusion was so powerful in Lester's mind that his body physically un-grew his fingers, toes and foot. In Lester's mind, however, it was the vengeful ghosts of the animals that were eating the parts of his body."

"But, how is it that Lester Haney died?" Dr. Kromley questioned.

"Very simple," Dr. Auguerre replied. "I was unable to reverse Lester's psychosomatic guilt response cycle and his spiral into nothingness continued until only his head remained. And, voila, that too disappeared on Monday. So here lies Lester Haney's remains, except nothing does remain. So his family is burying an empty coffin."

"Dr. Auguerre," Dr. Kromley replied, I have a question regarding your diagnosis."

"And what would that be?" Dr. Auguerre replied.

"Did you ever consider the possibility that animals actually do have ghosts? Dr. Kromley asked" and that they possibly do come back and avenge the wrongs that were done to them by humans?"

"I don't believe in ghosts, animal or otherwise," Dr. Auguerre replied laughing.

"I do," Dr. Kromley said solemnly, as he reached to shake Dr. Aguerre's hand and tell her "goodbye."

Dr. Auguerre gasped as she shook Dr. Kromley's hand. You're missing several fingers, Dr. Kromley," she said.

Dr. Kromley looked at Dr. Auguerre. "Yes," he said. "They weren't missing when I went to bed last night."

Members Only

The black Bentley smoothly cruised over the one lane bridge connecting Pembroke Island to the mainland. The Bentley, which I estimated to have cost in excess of three hundred-thousand dollars, was driven by a chauffeur named Albert, a fiftyish man not prone to conversation. For some reason, I presumed the designated role of anyone named Albert was to be a chauffeur. I'd seen too many 1940's movies, I suppose.

My host, Sir Jeffrey Tarvelle, had personally met me at the small airport half an hour earlier. While Albert drove, Sir Jeffrey and I sat in the back seat performing our own designated roles. Sir Jeffrey "amazed" me with grand stories of his famous hunts and the trophies he had taken. While Sir Jeffrey blathered on, I performed my designated role which was to reliably gush oos and ahs on cue. I actually found Sir Jeffrey and his stories very boring. That someone would go into the wilderness with a high powered rifle and kill an animal with the only intent being to add another creature's head to his trophy wall seemed barbaric and stupid.

And that was my opinion of Sir Jeffrey. My name is Ed Stansby, by the way. I'm a reporter and my editor assigned me the job of covering the grand opening of the Pembroke Island Hunt Club. We had to give them good press, he instructed, because these are very influential men and we must keep them happy. "There are no women in the hunt club?" I asked.

My editor scoffed, "Of course not. Women don't hunt." As a matter of logic, I knew women did hunt, but that same logic should have told me women would never be admitted to this ultra-exclusive private club.

We had driven another few miles when Albert announced, "We have arrived, sir." Albert didn't inform me we had arrived, but I had already figured that out on my own as I looked out the window at the massive, log lodge with the imposing sign hanging over the entrance. "Pembroke Island Hunt Club," it said. I don't need a chauffeur, I thought.

As I sat there I thought of my own car, a six year old Saturn which cost less than the Bentley's door Alert had just opened for me. Do poor people like me resent the rich, I wondered. Of course they do. On the other hand, I'd never buy a Bentley because it couldn't fit in my garage. Besides, I don't have a garage, so that's just one more problem I don't have to worry about.

Sir Jeffrey and I walked up the front steps to the main entrance. "Members Only," a sign said. This would probably be the only time in my life I would ever be here. We walked through the front door and into the lobby. It was a smaller room, decorated with the rich wood paneling one would expect to see in an exclusive lodge. I'd never been to an expensive lodge before, but that's what I imagined it would look like.

From the back of the lobby, two hallways leading in opposite directions guided people to their sleeping rooms. A doorway between the hallways led to the grand ballroom, which was where Sir Jeffrey was taking me. As we walked through that door, I was stunned by the enormity of this hall. It was here, Sir Jeffrey told me, that all activities take place and where we would be dining in several hours.

It was the décor of the room that made the greatest impression, however, it was not a good one. Animal heads of every species lined the walls. Cape buffalo, deer, bison, rhinoceros, elephant, there were even birds. "There are over two hundred and sixty trophies on those walls," he said. "Each member has at least one kill hanging on one of those four walls. You'll notice that under each trophy is the name of the member who killed that particular animal. You see this moose head," he said. "You see whose name is underneath it on the bronze plaque," he boasted. "Sir Jeffrey Tarvelle."

"Nice," I said, but not really thinking so.

"I took that moose in Canada, a record kill I might add. It's impressive, is it not," he said.

I was tempted to answer "no" but I needed my job. Besides, a reporter's job is to be objective. I was having a rough time of remaining so tonight however. "Yes," I agreed, "it is impressive," I lied. It was actually sick. You wouldn't think it was so impressive if you were one of the poor animals Sir Jeffrey, I thought.

"Look, old boy," he said, after an extended tour of the mausoleum aka dining room, "you go down to your room and freshen up and I'll meet you back here for a cocktail in half an hour. Albert has taken your bags so you needn't concern yourself with them."

As instructed, I walked down the hallway to my room and crashed, wondering how I arrived at this point in my life. I lay on the bed for a while, and at the appointed time, I returned to the dining room to meet Sir Jeffrey. I spotted him immediately, standing with several other members and gesturing wildly, probably describing how gallant he was as he brought down some unsuspecting beast with his favorite gun. He waved at me. "Come over here, Eddie," he yelled.

I walked up to the group of middle aged and older men as a waiter scurried over to take my drink order. "He'll have a martini," my host told the waiter. "Make it extra dry."

"Thank you, Sir Jeffrey," I said. "It was just what I wanted." That was the only truthful remark I'd made since meeting this dull, overbearing man. Besides, a martini would fortify me for the evening to come. I was already contemplating having a second one and the waiter hadn't yet made it to the bar to order the first. But, it didn't take long for him to return, and as Sir Jeffrey jabbered away, I took a couple of swallows of expensive gin and looked at the sea of white tablecloths around us. Each table had six chairs. Every member would be here tonight, Sir Jeffrey said proudly. Full house!" He exclaimed.

Things had become a little blurry by the time we sat down for dinner. I was seated at the head table next to Sir Jeffrey, though I don't know why. It made me quite uncomfortable to sit there staring out at two hundred and fifty wealthy men whose cheapest pair of shoes cost more than my weekly salary. Ignoring my self-assigned two drink limit, I had finished my third martini when dinner was served.

It was at that time I thought I noticed Sir Jeffrey's prize moose head move, if only slightly. Incredible martinis, I thought. As I looked again, however, the moose's head had turned completely to its right, apparently conversing with the Cape water buffalo which was shaking its head up and down in agreement. A Bengal tiger's head four trophies down was looking to its left, joining the conversation. Whatever was being said, the tiger too was in agreement. It was very odd, but what was even more bizarre, though the animals' mouths were obviously speaking words I couldn't hear any sounds.

Apparently, I was the only one in the room who had noticed this strange conversation taking place between disembodied animal heads hanging on the wall across the room.

"Another martini, sir," the waiter inquired.

"No, thank you very much," I replied. "I've had quite enough to drink." I got to the business of eating my dinner, ignoring the talking animal heads directly opposite where I sat. What I thought I'd seen was the result of three generous martinis, I concluded.

After two bites of food, my curiosity got the best of me and I glanced at the heads once again. But now, all the animal heads were moving and talking in what had become an animalian gabfest. All the animal heads on all four walls had become invigorated, moving about in an excited state.

My editor had warned me about my drinking. "Don't ever drink while on assignment," he'd lectured. He was right, I thought. I'm out of control. I'm hallucinating. Oh good lord, the heads are floating around, moving up and down the walls and chatting with particular friends, I guessed. I don't feel that drunk, I told myself. No really.

I wondered if I should mention this rather strange phenomenon taking place all around us. No one else seemed to notice anything was amiss. I looked back at my plate, trying to force myself to take another bite of food. "This is not happening," I said under my breath.

"Pardon me," Sir Jeffrey said.

"Oh nothing, sir," I replied. "I was just remarking what a great martini they make here at the club."

"Oh yeah," he said. "Too bad you can't come to the club more often," he said. "Members only, you know."

"Yes, it's a shame," I said. "Well, maybe I can become a member someday," I said, knowing it would never happen.

"I don't think so," he replied, condescendingly.

What a smug jerk, I thought, as I looked back at my plate glumly. His answer made me feel badly and infuriated me. I'm going to tell Sir Jeffrey exactly what kind of jerk he is, I decided. "Sir Jeffrey," I said, turning to him, "you're a real….." I stopped myself. Sir Jeffrey Tarvelle was gone.

"Where is he?" I blurted out.

"Where is who, sir?" the waiter asked, as he walked up to my table.

"Sir Jeffrey," I said. "He was here a moment ago, but now he's gone. He couldn't have left that quickly and without my noticing."

The waiter looked at me, a sly smile on his face. "Sir Jeffrey is here, sir. Look around the room a bit."

"What?" I said.

"Look around the room sir," the waiter said, his mischievous smile becoming wider.

It was then I saw a huge moose standing in the back of the room looking up at the wall. I recoiled from the table, nearly falling out of my chair. Sir Jeffry's head was on the wall where the moose's head had been.

In shock, I looked at the waiter. He was smiling triumphantly. "That's Sir Jeffrey's trophy moose looking his trophy Sir Jeffrey," he giggled. It's happening," he said.

"What was happening?" I asked, as I looked around the room to see the most horrifying of spectacles. Pembroke Island Hunt Club members were vanishing from their chairs and their heads were replacing the animal heads on the dining room walls. Ghostly animals with their heads reattached to their bodies were appearing in the room. It was over in less than a minute. All four walls were now populated by human heads.

The waiter and I walked amongst the animals as we crossed the room to look at the new trophies on the wall. There was Sir Jeffrey's head, not so boastful now. As before, the bronze plaque underneath it read, "Sir Jeffrey Tarvelle."

"Isn't that lovely?" the waiter asked. "Each of the members's heads ended up where his trophy animal head been earlier, and with his name on the bronze plaque below it. The animals got even," he said.

"I can see that. Why didn't the animals do the same to you and me and the rest of the help?" I asked.

The waiter smiled and replied, "Members only."

Dinosaur Séance

"Welcome. I am Madame Juliette Cocteau," the woman announced to the three fidgety people sitting at the circular table. "You are here because you wish to communicate with your beloved little friends who have gone before us. It is my function to facilitate that process."

Madame Cocteau, a medium, has the ability to communicate with the dead. A white table cloth covered the table and its center sat three tall white candles in a triangular arrangement. Madame Cocteau lighted them.

The three people sitting at the table included Dr. Alfred Knaufstedder, a self-described Chimerical Paleontologist, Loretta Boborich, an anxious widow from Trenton, and Fred Laurentine, a shadowy character who volunteered no details other than his name, if indeed he actually had.

Madame Cocteau, a large boned, heavy woman in her late fifties, provided an overview of how each person should conduct him or herself during the séance and what might be expected as the evening progressed. "Now I would like you to give me a brief summary of who you are and why you are here," she said, with a somewhat patronizing smile.

Dr. Knaufstedder, a tall, ungainly individual with gray hair and a thin black moustache, was the first to speak. "There is no way to know what we don't know, that infinity of knowledge that man does not possess. Much has vanished since the earth was born and even more waits to be revealed in the future. But, I'm an impatient soul. I want to know everything now, even though I realize that without the technology which is yet to be invented, I cannot fathom what will be discovered in the far off future.

Therefore, I wish to explore the possibilities a séance might offer as a way to learn about the past, or at least the part of the past in which I am interested. I am the only practitioner of a branch of science known as Chimerical Paleontology, a field which specializes in the study of ancient animals which were never known to exist. You might say that is an impossible task. How can one study animals which never existed? There is no physical evidence such as a fossil record. There are no eye witness reports. There is nothing. However, I believe that by means of a séance, I can communicate with the spirits of long dead, hitherto unknown creatures. I hope to find out who they are, what they looked like, and how they lived."

"Thank you, Doctor," Madame Cocteau interjected. "Now, Mrs. Boborich, would you please tell us about yourself?"

"Please, call me, Loretta," the stylishly dressed woman responded. "I am a recently widowed housewife from New Jersey. Although I loved my husband, he is not the one with whom I wish to contact in the afterlife. I terribly miss my little white poodle, Mimi. If I could reach her, I would be so grateful."

"I see," Madame Cocteau smiled. "What about you, Mr. Laurentine? What is it you wish to accomplish tonight?"

"I need to talk to a dead guy named Alfonso Maricomo," was all he said.

There was silence as the three other people at the table contemplated Mr. Laurentine. That he had the stereotypical appearance of a gangster or street thug was not missed by the small group."Why do you wish to contact Mr. Maricomo, Mr. Laurentine?" Madame Cocteau asked.

"He put something some place and I need to find out where," Mr. Laurentine answered.

"Do you wish to share what you are trying to locate, Mr. Laurentine?" asked Madame Cocteau.

"Not really," he answered.

"Alright," Madame Cocteau said, with a bewildered look on her face. "I want to thank everyone for that information."

Madame Cocteau was wearing a dark red velvet dress which, coincidentally or not, matched the velvet wall coverings. At this point her assistant, a thin, black-haired woman in a dark green velvet gown, entered the room. As she stood somberly near the door observing the group, the three séance participants sitting with Madame Cocteau pondered if a smile had ever appeared on her face.

Madame Cocteau introduced her. "This is my colleague, Miss Hubenswain."

Dr. Knaufstedder and Loretta Boborich nodded at the woman. Fred Laurentine did not.

"We shall now prepare for our séance," Madame Cocoteau announced. "First, if you have a cell phone, please turn it off. The spirits are annoyed by ringing and buzzing noises. Miss Hubenswain, will you please light the incense? Thank you dear. If you have a sweater or coat, you may wish to put it on. Sometimes the spirits cause the temperature to drop. Also, when you ask the spirits questions, they may answer with a bump or a tapping noise, or perhaps a breeze across your face. They may also answer through me, asking that I give you a message. Are there any questions, group?"

"I have one question, Madame Cocteau," answered Dr. Knaufstedder. "I have heard that sometimes evil spirits invade a séance. Is that true?"

"On rare occasions, an unwelcome entity might 'crash' a séance," Madame Cocteau replied. "However, if that occurs, I shall handle him." Dr. Knaufsteder nodded approvingly.

Loretta Boborich placed an 8 1/2 by 11 photo of Mimi on the table. "Who's the mutt?" Fred Laurentine asked gruffly."

"She's not a mutt," Loretta replied coolly. "She's my little, Mimi, if it's any of your business."

Laurentine rolled his eyes, feigning boredom.

"I wish you luck in the séance, Loretta," Dr. Knaufstedder said consolingly. She nodded in appreciation.

"Please, let us join our hands together," Madame Cocteau requested.

"Is that really necessary?" Mr. Laurentine asked. "I don't want to hold hands with no guy."

"We only need to hold hands until the first spirit visits us," Madame Cocteau said, "then we can break the circle. If Loretta wouldn't mind, you may switch places and sit between her and me, Mr. Laurentine."

"That will be fine," Loretta said, as she rose from her chair and sat down next to Dr. Knaufstedder.

"Join hands now, group," Madame Cocteau said, as she looked at each person individually. "We are ready now." She looked toward Miss Hubenswain who immediately switched off the lights. The three candles were now the only light in the room.

"Now group," Madame Cocteau said, "think of that pet or person you wish to contact. In your case, Dr. Kanufstedder, try to envision those unknown creatures that prowled the earth long before man appeared." She began to chant. "Oh spirits who have preceded us to that beauteous land of the afterlife, come before us now. Speak to us. Show us your love."

"I don't love Alfonso," Laurentine interjected. "I'm the one what put him where he is."

"Please Mr. Laurentine," Madame Cocteau snapped in an annoyed tone, concentrate on the séance and do not speak."

"Come to us now," Madame Cocteau demanded sharply." She slapped the table twice with her right hand. "Come now," she stated firmly.

Suddenly, a tiny, white toy poodle was dancing around in front of Loretta Boborich. She gasped with joy as she picked up the little dog up and hugged it. "Mimi!" she exclaimed. "Oh Mimi!"

Loretta cuddled Mimi while silence returned to the room. Dr. Knaufstedder and Fred Laurentine sat quietly and waited. Madame Cocteau stared at her folded hands resting on the table, seemingly contemplating her left thumb which, for unspecified reasons, was pointed upward and slowly rotating. Dr. Knaufstedder assumed the revolving digit was part of the séance ritual. Mr. Laurentine concluded Madame Cocteau was a dizzy broad.

"I command you to appear before us now," Madame Cocteau called into the darkness of the room.

A bizarre, pygmy-like creature resembling a miniature Tyrannosaurus Rex abruptly scampered across the table to Dr. Knaufstedder's folded hands and promptly bit him on his left knuckle. "Ouch, he screamed, as blood oozed from his wound. Mimi leapt from Loretta's arms, intent on attacking the disagreeable Triassic pip-squeak. However, the spry dinosaurian fingerling jumped to the floor and headed toward the spooky Miss Hubenswain who was screaming hysterically as she hiked up her skirt and began running round the room.

Aghast, Mr. Laurentine quietly watched as the wailing Miss Hubenswain ran around the room followed by the tiny growling dinosaur which was followed by the yipping toy poodle, Mimi. Mr. Laurentine finally commented, "I love a parade."

Another visitor from the Triassic age suddenly appeared, although this one was much larger and more colorful. Its fat, bright yellow lower body was the size of three hippopotamuses. The monster's long, bright yellow neck supported a bright red head with glowing green eyes surrounded by yellow scleras.

In order to not bump against the séance parlor ceiling, the animal had to bend its neck and lower its head, consequently positioning it face to face with Mr. Laurentine. Fortunately, he was dull-witted and lethargic, the dinosaur, that is. Unfortunately, he chose that exact moment to relieve himself, the dinosaur, that it is, and a three foot high, two hundred pound heap of reeking dung appeared behind him.

The powerful stench enveloped the room, somehow adding to Miss Hubenswain's hysteria. She ran more wildly now, her two pursuers close behind. Mr. Laurentine, annoyed the large creature looking at him wasn't house-broken, slapped the offending animal across his face. It burped loudly, simultaneously expelling a greenish-yellow mass onto the table in front of Mr. Laurentine.

It was at that inconvenient time that Alfonso Maricomo made his ghostly appearance. He was a ghastly looking man and the knife handle sticking from the middle of his chest was not the most stylish of accessories. "Where did you put it?" Mr. Laurentine screamed.

Mr. Maricomo let out a ghoulish rattle, the best guffaw he could muster with a knife sticking through his lungs. "I'll never tell you," he replied, in a bitter, hollow cackle.

With that, he pulled the knife from his chest and advanced toward Mr. Laurentine. "Your turn to die now, Freddie," he squawked. Mr. Laurentine jumped from his chair and ran toward the door however he quickly discovered what Miss Hubenswain already had. The door was locked.

Mr. Laurentine had no option other than join Miss Hubenswain in her panicked flight around the room. Oddly, he assumed his chances for survival would be better than Miss Hubenswain's if he could out-scream her as they ran. Mr. Maricomo ran close behind, cursing in a hollow rasp and swiping his bloody knife at Mr. Laurentine's backside.

Loretta Boborich, concerned for Mimi's safety, decided she should join the orbital race to retrieve her beloved toy poodle. Standing at the ready, she watched as Miss Hubenswain went squealing past followed by the snarling teeny dinosaur followed by the yipping Mimi. Then she made her move, jumping into the unhinged circular line-up just in front of Mr. Laurentine being pursued by the most assuredly dead Mr. Maricomo.

Madame Cocteau, realizing the séance had gotten well out of control, stood up and yelled, "thank you all for coming to visit us, but it is time for you to leave." She clapped her hands twice. The spirit visitors ignored her.

Madame Cocteau was now becoming worried. "Your attention please," she declared assertively. "I order you to vacate the premises and return to the afterlife." Again, the ghostly beings paid her no heed. Things were too interesting here, they must have thought.

The séance had deteriorated into total chaos and Madame Cocteau looked quite unnerved, thought Dr. Knaufstedder. He was aroused by Madame Cocteau's "damsel in distress" appearance. Getting up from his chair, he quickly rounded the table to where Madame Cocteau stood. Breathing heavily, he said, "Juliette, I am madly in love with you. I must have you now."

The horrified Madame Cocteau looked up at the tall, clumsy man panting in her face. "Oh, my god," she gasped. Then she fainted.

*

Afterword:

- When Madame Cocteau fainted, the connection with the dead was instantly terminated and the séance ended.
- Dr. Knaufstedder succeeded in identifying over twenty previously unknown types of dinosaurs. He sketched the two dinosaurs which had been in the room and luckily collected the two hundred pound stool sample remaining

after the dinosaurs' departure. Even better, outside Madame Cocteau's home was a huge collection of dinosaur footprints left by those creatures not able to get into the séance room.

- Loretta Boborich was so happy she was able to see Mimi. A side benefit was that she enjoyed running around the room after Mimi so much that she is now a regular participant in the New York Marathon.

- Mr. Lorentine left the hoodlum business, happy to be alive after his close call with the knife wielding Mr. Maricomo. Unfortunately, Mr. Laurentine did lose a major portion of his right cheek when Mr. Maricomo got in a lucky hack with his knife. As a result, when Mr. Laurentine is sitting in a chair, he leans thirty degrees to his right. Mr. Laurentine now works as an executive for a large bank where he can legally steal money from customers.

- Miss Hubenswain now works at the City Zoo in the reptile house.

- Madame Cocteau sold her séance business to a hedge fund which sells guaranteed admissions to heaven. The mortgages on these heavenly claims are bundled and sold to pension funds, city retirement plans, and any other large organizations capable of ruining peoples' lives in their senior years.

HULLABALOO

Walter the Fruit Fly

"Huh." I mumbled, as I struggled to focus my alcohol blurred eyes. "What? I can't hear what you're saying." I stared over the glass forest of empty ginger colored beer bottles trying to see all the way to the opposite end of the kitchen table. But it was much too far, and my bleary eyes beheld only a fuzzy smear of that distant horizon. Wonder how the weather is over there. "Looks like rain's comin," was my forecast.

My present circumstances and my inebriated condition were due to yet another low point in my life. I'd lost my third girlfriend in as many months. I don't mean I'd somehow misplaced her. She dumped me. That's why I was sitting alone in my kitchen trying to forget my troubles. I normally don't drink very much, but my self-pity over-rode my sense of propriety that evening.

"Can you see me?" a raspy little voice screamed. "I'm only four feet away from you. Lookee here, I'm waving my arms, all six of them. Can you see me now?"

It seemed like one of those pointless cell phone conversations in which the only thing concluded is that neither caller hears the other. "Can you hear me now? Too bad. Oh well, nice talking with you anyway, Joe. Goodbye."

"Hey, I moved closer to you. I'm two feet in front of you. Can you see me now?"

Squinting mightily, I strained my eyes. I could see something, tiny though it was. It was some kind of bug, I realized. Because of my besotted condition, it hadn't yet occurred to me that a talking bug was a little out of the ordinary. "Yeah, I see you," I replied.

"I went on a diet and lost weight," the bug said. "That's probably why you couldn't see me."

"Oh," I replied, resentful that he had success on his diet while I gained seven pounds on mine. "What do you want with me?" I asked, begrudgingly. "And, how is it you can talk?" I added, finally taking note of the fact that I was conversing with an insect.

"Jealous, aren't you," he said triumphantly, flaunting his tiny, stick-like figure and sleek see-through wings.

I ignored his taunts and tried to make sense of what was going on. "What do you want from me?" I asked. "And, what kind of insect are you?

"Didn't you take biology in high school?" he asked. I'm a fruit fly. I've noticed you have a lot of trouble with the opposite sex. I had the same problem and I got drunk just like you did. My name is Walter, by the way."

"Well I had a reason to have a couple of beers," I challenged him. "I've lost my girlfriend. That's three of them now."

"So did I," he answered. "But, I got rejected twenty-two times," he said. "So I got drunk."

"Fruit flies can't get drunk," I said. "That's ridiculous."

"Not!" Walter the obnoxious fruit fly exclaimed. "They did a study," he continued. "They found that rejected fruit flies and lots of other species turn to alcohol when they are spurned by their lovers. Being brushed off twenty-two times is a lot of frustration. I had a right and moral obligation to become intoxicated. But, you, three times rebuffed. That's no hill for a climber, you big sissy."

"You best be careful, little fella,' I said. "I could set one of these beer bottles on your little head and it would be all over for you."

"Oh, you scare me," he said. "Of course, you could go out to the bar tonight and brag to your buddies that you beat up a little fruit fly that doesn't weigh as much as the cap on your beer bottle?"

I ignored his comment, but feeling some empathy for him, asked why he thought he was spurned so many times.

"It's my eyes. They're white."

"So what's your point?"

"Fruit fly eyes are red, at least most of them are."

"So what happened to you? How'd you end up with white eyes?"

"I'm a victim," he said.

"Aren't we all?" I replied.

"No, I really am. This high school kid was doing a biology experiment on naturally occurring fruit fly mutations with white eyes. I'm one of the white-eyed mutants. No self-respecting female fruit fly wants me."

I felt really badly for the little guy. "What can I do for you to make you happy?" I asked.

"I'm afraid it's too late," he said.

"It's never too late. I'll help you find a mate," I promised. I wasn't sure I could actually deliver on that commitment, but I had to try. The poor guy was really upset.

"But, it is too late," he countered. "You see, I'm dead," he announced.

"If you're dead, how can you be standing there talking to me?" I asked.

"I'm a ghost, the ghost of the former Walter the fruit fly. My name is also Walter, of course."

I must be really drunk, I thought. I'm sitting here talking to an insect who insists he's the ghost of a mutant fruit fly. "So, what do you want from me, Wally?" I asked.

"All I want now is some self-respect. If you would hold a funeral and wake for me, I'd feel a lot better about myself. Do you think you could do that?" he asked.

"Yeah, sure," I said, not really thinking through the ramifications of that promise. But, as I pondered the thought of staging a funeral for a dead fruit fly, it suddenly occurred to me that it was not a rational thing to do. I immediately had second thoughts, but when I looked back in Walter's direction, he was gone. His tiny ghost had vanished.

I got up from my chair and looked around the kitchen. I even called his name. But, there was no further sign of Walter. I decided that I must have gone to sleep on the table after my fourth beer and dreamed this bizarre incident. It couldn't possibly have occurred. I forgot about the whole thing and went to bed. It never happened, I thought, as I turned out the light on my nightstand.

At exactly midnight, I was awakened by loud bumping noises in the kitchen. I jumped out of my bed, thinking an intruder had broken into the house. As I crept into the kitchen with my golf putter resting on my shoulder ready to strike, I immediately spied the cause of the ruckus. All the apples and oranges from the fruit bowl were scattered on the kitchen floor. "How did that happen?" I grumbled.

But, it was then I noticed the ghostly warning on the counter. Spelled out in grapes was the name "Walter." I recoiled in terror, stepping backwards out of the kitchen. As I regained my composure, I decided Wally's message was a reminder of my promise to stage a funeral and wake for him.

"Alright," I screamed, at no one in particular. "I'll have your funeral and wake tomorrow." I went back to bed but couldn't sleep, kept awake by the planning I was doing for Wally's funeral.

The next day was Saturday. As I didn't have a body, I had no choice but to have a closed coffin funeral. I painted a toothpick box black and set it in the center of the kitchen table. I made a point of inviting all the neighbors that morning. Unfortunately, no one came.

"You're having a funeral for a fruit fly?" they would ask, a look of astonishment on their faces. However, their bewilderment soon turned to fear. I could hear people clicking the locks when they closed their doors.

None of the neighbors have spoken to me since, nor do they dare even make eye contact with me now.

Walter the fruit fly did me no favors. I hope he is resting peacefully in fruit fly heaven or wherever dearly departed fruit flies end up.

Harry the Cynical Cat

"Meow. Yeah, I'm a cat. You got a problem with that? My name's Harry. Yeah, I know. That's a stupid name for a cat. But my owner, Charles Benson, he's stupid too. Do you expect a stupid owner not to name his cat a stupid name? Couldn't he call me some normal cat name? Bill would be nice. He should have named me Bill.

Oh yeah, not being a detail oriented cat, I forgot to tell you. I'm dead. I also didn't tell Charles I'm dead. It wasn't that I forgot. It's just that Charles is a motivational speaker, one of these terminally optimistic, ultra-positive people. To maintain balance in his little world and to practice his motivational speeches, he relies on me for cynicism and negativity. I'm very good at both of those. If he knew I was dead, it would kill him.

Even though I said he's stupid, he's really not. I just have to say those kinds of things and bitch at the state of the universe in general because that's my personality. I'm actually a very nice cat, kind of a feline knight, if you will. I go around the neighborhood doing good deeds. But, I can't let that part of my personality be widely known. Cynical cats don't do good deeds.

You see, although I do good things, I pretend to do bad things like coughing up fur balls, eating little birds, crapping in people's sand boxes, and yowling because I'm having glorious sex with some slutty little Siamese. No, it's not true that Siamese cats have two attached bodies. Urban myth. You're thinking of Siamese twins.

That I'm cynical and negative but secretly a loving, caring cat makes me complex. I always wanted to be complex because I once saw a movie that had a complex person in it. That's who I want to be like, I thought to myself. Complex people always do contradictory, annoying things and irritate everyone. Don't you love that? But, they always come through by redeeming themselves with some heroic act. That's me. I'm a jerk but also very nice. That's makes me complex. I can be introspective and brood and people will think I'm a deep thinker with solutions for the world's problems.

Alright, I admit I have issues. I also admit that yesterday I did a really bad thing. Hopefully, writing about this misdeed will expunge some of my guilt. Not! See what I mean about issues?

Anyway, I was just finishing my morning rounds of the neighborhood where I'm pretending to be doing "cat things." I was sitting on a tree branch looking into a robin's nest at the five little ones. Mommy and Daddy Robin flew away thinking I'd eat them if they stayed. The neighbors thought I'd eat the baby birds. But, I didn't come there to eat anyone. The baby birds were malnourished. There hasn't been much rain. The ground's too hard for Mommy and Daddy Robin to dig for worms. "Hang on baby birds," I said. "I'll be right back. I have to go down on the ground and dig some worms for you."

See, that's what I do. I help those in need. The ground was hard but I got three worms. I had to put them in my mouth because cats don't have opposable thumbs. That's another complaint I have. Cats should have opposable thumbs. Good Lord, the worms tasted awful. It was hard to climb back up to the nest. "I'm getting too old for this," I told myself. "Here you go little guys," I said. Baby robins just love worms. "Have a nice day, guys."

It was almost ten o'clock and I had to get back to the house for my weekly appointment. Just before I died, Charles hired someone to analyze me and straighten out my personality. He says I've become too negative lately. He doesn't understand that he needs me to be that way. I have to counter-balance his warped positivity. I wonder if he would be psychoanalyzing me if he knew I was dead. Personally, I feel that being dead adds to the mystique of my complex nature.

Speaking of names, not that we are, this person Charles hired calls herself Chinchilla, the Cat Whisperer. Feast your literary eyes on that handle. Why do all these animal shrinks think they have to whisper? I'm hard of hearing so when Chinchilla whispers to me, all I hear are her dentures clicking and a death rattle gurgle coming from somewhere deep inside her dark, cave-like throat. Her thick red lips move with contorted twists and stretches, enunciating silent words in a heavy Romanian accent. The point is, I can't understand a word she isn't saying. "Meow," I always say to her, smiling my best cat smile. That makes her think I'm making progress. That'll be the day. How can someone named after a rodent think she's going solve my mental malfunctions?

After I went through my little door and into the kitchen, I heard Charles talking so I knew she was there. She's never late. As I walked across the living room and jumped up on the couch, she saw me. She always sits on the stool by the couch and looks directly into my eyes and whispers to me. If that sounds weird, that's only because it is.

"Oh, here's Harry, now," she said. "Hello, Harry. Did you miss me, dear?"

Of course, I can hear her while she's actually talking and not lip syncing in her bizarre, shrink whisper.

Hell no, I didn't miss you. Don't they have cats in Romania you can whisper to? Of course, she can't hear me because I'm only thinking that.

"Charles," she said, "why don't you leave Harry and me alone for a little while?" Charles nodded and walked out. She sat down on the stool and as he walked out of the room, she watched him leave. I was sitting on the couch wishing she'd leave.

"Harry," she whispered, "how do you feel today?" I could hardly hear her. "Did the little green hyper-energy pills help?" She doesn't know I fed half the bottle of pills to the Schnauzer next door. He somehow jumped the seven foot backyard fence and forced himself on a Great Dane in heat. I got a kick out of that. I understand the Great Dane did too.

"Talk to me, Harry," she said, in her thick Romanian accent. "Tell me you're going to be happy and positive. Surprise me." I was going to surprise her, alright. I had this planned for a week.

I moved closer and looked straight at her. "Ruff, ruff," I barked, in my most vicious German Shepherd imitation. "Ruff, ruff."

A look of complete horror came over Chinchilla's face. She never heard a cat bark before. "Ruff, ruff," I barked again, and started snarling like a rabid dog.

The poor woman was breathing heavily and had no idea how to react to this frightening predicament. "Harry," she gasped weakly, "cats don't bark."

"Oink, Oink!" I squealed at her loudly. "Oink, Oink, Oink!" In her experience as feline shrink, she apparently had never come across a barking cat, let alone one who oinked at her.

She stood up and backed away, making the sign of the cross three times.

"Moo, Moo!" I said, glaring at her. "Moooo!" I added the longer moo to theatrically emphasize the bovine intensity. I thought she'd find that very scary. She did.

"Mary and all the saints, protect me. St. Jude, protect me. The devil has possessed one of God's creatures and he is here in this house."

"Quack, quack, quack," I said authoritatively, and jumped from the couch onto the stool where she'd been sitting. "Quack, quack!"

"Oh God!" she shrieked. "Forgive me for all my sins. The devil is among us." She crossed herself three more times, for extra insurance I guessed. Then she ran out of the living room screaming.

"Mr. Benson!" she screeched in terror. "Help, Mr. Benson!"

"What is it Ms. Chinchilla?" I heard Charles ask the panic stricken woman.

"Harry barked at me," she said, trying to catch her breath. "He oinked, quacked and went moo at me too. Harry's possessed by the devil, Mr. Benson."

"What!" Charles exclaimed, as they walked back into the living room. "Harry doesn't bark." By Charles' stating only that I didn't bark may have left Ms. Chinchilla with the impression that oinking, quacking and mooing was my normal mode of communication.

Charles stood with his back toward me, comforting the bawling Ms. Chinchilla who was warily looking past his shoulder at me.

She watched me closely as I stood on the couch looking back at her. Then my body slowly rose into the air, floating eighteen inches above the couch.

"Oh, my God!" she howled. "He's a demon, an evil spirit." She turned and ran for the front door, again making the sign of the cross three times before she reached it. She pulled the door open and ran through.

Goodbye, Chinchilla, I'm thinking, a feline smirk on my face.

I was back down and standing on the couch before Charles saw my little prank. He came over and sat down next to me. He stroked my back. I purred and looked up at him.

"You're a good cat, Harry," he said. "I don't know what's wrong with that woman. You'd think she'd seen a ghost."

Bugged

I was sitting in Aunt Melba's Country Kitchen somewhere in Oklahoma. Although the place was crowded, I walked in just as a middle aged couple vacated the booth at which I now sat. I was by myself, and even though every other seat in the place was occupied, I still felt a little guilty taking a four person booth. That I did so would not turn out to be a good thing.

I make it a point to be a very polite and considerate person. As I sat there alone in my booth with only a cup of coffee on the table, a major guilt trip was coming over me. The yet unseated and increasingly impatient customers were casting annoyed looks my way as they whispered to one another. This added to my considerable discomfort that I was occupying someone else's seat. Actually, sitting alone in the four person booth meant that I was occupying four peoples' seats.

I also remembered that during an earlier stop I heard a bug flying and buzzing around my right ear. I waved my hand in a swatting motion to shoo the bug away. But somehow, the pest landed on my right ear and crawled inside. My index finger immediately went inside my right ear in pursuit of the intruder. I thought I plucked it out of there. Then I got in the car and continued my journey.

But now, I felt a stirring deep inside that same right ear, not that it could be a different right ear obviously. It was definitely moving around in there. Both the bug and I realized it was out of reach for my index finger. And then, the most shocking thing occurred. The bug spoke to me.

"Larry. Larry." it called to me. "We have to talk."

Warily, I looked around the restaurant at the other customers. I don't know why I did that because no could possibly have heard the bug or notice it was attempting to engage in conversation with me. But, for some reason, I felt I must conceal the bug's presence and keep its conversation secret from the other customers. It's none of their business what's going on inside my right ear, I concluded.

At first, I didn't answer the bug, pretending to ignore it. But how can one ignore a creature, although ever so tiny, speaking with an authoritative voice from inside one's own ear?

"Larry!" it screamed at me, in a tone of great irritation. I know you hear me, Larry. Answer me."

I looked cautiously at the other customers to make sure they weren't watching then cupped my hand over my mouth. "What do you want?" I asked.

No one seemed to notice my speaking into my right hand folded over my mouth.

"What did you say, Larry?" it screamed. "Speak up, will you."

Unbelievable, I thought, of all the bugs in all the world, as the saying goes, I get the one that's hard of hearing.

As inconspicuously as possible, I again moved my right hand from my coffee cup to cover my mouth. "I said what do you want?" And again, I talked very softly to avoid drawing attention to myself.

"I told you we have to talk, Larry. Is that so difficult for you to comprehend?"

In all honesty, the fact that a bug was the one asking me that question did make it a bit difficult to comprehend. To make the situation even more difficult, although I had never come across a talking bug prior to this unpleasant encounter, I began to form the impression that this particular bug was not going to be my friend.

"What do we have to talk about?" I replied, trying to conceal my moving lips and words so my fellow diners would not think I was crazy and having a conversation with some imaginary, invisible friend. Also, I was trying to figure if I was speaking to a male or female bug. It seemed that identifying the gender of my uninvited coffee partner was important.

"You know very well what we need to talk about, Larry," the bug screamed in exasperation.

For some reason, the negative tone of the abusive bug greatly riled me. "What? What is it we need to discuss?" I blurted out in frustration. I inadvertently neglected to lower my voice and cover my mouth to conceal my abrasive reply from the other restaurant customers.

Unfortunately my unintentional outburst, though mild, startled my fellow diners, several of whom were now casting worrisome looks my way. They were probably wondering if I had weapons. I did have a tube of chap-stick in my pocket but I didn't think that counted. Although, come to think of it, I recalled reading some place that a tube of cherry chap-stick was used in a jail break in Pittsburgh. Mine was regular chap-stick, however. No way was regular chap-stick a weapon. The diners at the two tables nearest me hurriedly finished their food and left.

"They think I'm nuts," I thought. Mable the waitress later told me that I had a wild look in my eye.

For some reason, I decided if I repeated my question to the bug with a lowered voice and my hand covering my mouth, everything would be okay and the customers would overlook my frantic outburst.

"I mean, what do we have to talk about?" I replied once again, but in a more hushed and civil tone this time.

"Well if you don't know, I'm not going to tell you," the bug responded in a huff.

At that point, I knew I was speaking to a female bug. That's what females always do. At least, that is how most of my conversations with females seem to go.

"What exactly do you want?" I asked again, with my cupped hand pressed against my mouth. Unfortunately, after attracting the attention of the other restaurant patrons with my earlier outburst, several of them were watching me closely. They were picking up that I was communicating with someone, probably an imaginary invisible friend, in which case they no doubt concluded I was crazy. The local police were probably racing to Aunt Melba's at this very moment with a straitjacket and a gallon of mace.

"Oh! Men!" she replied, with great irritation.

"And I'm not Larry. Stop calling me Larry," I lied to her. I thought I could get rid of her by convincing her I was someone else and she had crawled into the wrong ear. But, my weak ploy failed to trick her. I didn't think bugs had that big a brain and therefore would be easy to trick. This did not turn out to be the case.

"Stop it Larry!" she screamed angrily. "The same old Larry. You'll never change, will you Larry?"

"What? Am I the father of one of your children, or something?" I replied cleverly, and quietly.

"Larry!" she screamed angrily. "Don't talk to me like I was born last week. Actually," she added, "strike that. I was born last week, come to think of it."

I pondered that, concluding she must have died when she was a human and come back as a bug. Why did she come back to me?

"Besides," she added, "my larvae just hatched and I had four hundred thousand, three hundred and fifty seven kids. You think you're man enough for that, Larry? Ha, ha, ha. I hardly think so," she emphasized hurtfully.

Then she said, and this was really painful for me, "And I didn't name any of them Larry." She stressed that point triumphantly.

"Oh, and I'm supposed to care?" I replied, trying to hide my hurt feelings. "Besides that, I told you I'm not Larry," I insisted.

I think every customer in the restaurant was watching me now. They were whispering to each other and pointing at me. "The rude guy who kept four people standing while he drank his measly coffee is a nut job," they were saying.

"You see, Larry, there you go again," the bug persevered. "Like I said, the same old Larry. Always ignoring the facts. Larry, Larry. What will I ever do with you?" she questioned sarcastically.

I pondered that. She spoke with such authority that it made me wonder if she actually did have the power to make some sort of disposition of my future. That frightened me.

She continued, returning to the issue of whether I was the father of her children. "Let's face it, Larry. The only kid you ever fathered was back when you were in eighth grade. One kid. Ha, ha, ha. Give me a break, Larry."

"Yeah, but it was with the assistant principal," I boasted.

"I know that, Larry. But, you were eighteen at the time," she cruelly reminded me, purposely bringing up the fact that I was something of a slow learner.

"You were a slow learner, weren't you Larry?" she sneered, further driving home her painful rebuttal.

"I had issues," I replied.

"You've always had issues," she gleefully countered.

"Look, what's your name……," I began to respond before she rudely cut me off.

"Phyllis! I'm Phyllis, Larry," she replied angrily. "Don't think that little 'I forget' trick of yours is going to work this time, Larry. If you think that, you are a slower learner than even I give you credit for," she skillfully jabbed.

"Alright," I snapped back in a loud whisper into my right hand, "this is getting us nowhere. Exactly what do you want?" I insisted.

"I just want to let you know that you're a real jerk, Larry. Every one of our four hundred thousand three hundred and fifty-seven kids is going to know that too. You thought you were so cool when you were a moth. You had those racing stripes painted on your wings. None of the other girls knew it was make-up but I did. I still devoted my life to you even though I knew you wore make-up. You and those racing stripes on your wings, Larry. You got every innocent little moth on her back on the nearest leaf. And the drinking. You promised you'd stop. How many times did I find you passed out by a dandelion which you had sucked dry of its hallucinogenic joy juice?"

"I don't remember any of this," I insisted. And truly, I didn't. But how did she know about my eighth grade debacle? And what about the other things she knew about me? Could she have gotten it off the internet?

Suddenly, I felt movement inside my ear. She's crawling out. Thank god, she's coming out of my ear! Then there was fluttering and buzzing outside my ear as she jumped off my right lobe and into the air.

Somehow, and I don't know how it was actually possible, she managed to project her miniature authoritative voice beyond established audibility limits as specified in every physics sound wave chart. She screamed a profanity at me with such powerful volume that any audibility meter in the room would be instantly destroyed. However, I didn't believe Aunt Melba's Country Kitchen actually had one of those devices on the premises.

"Screw you, Larry!" she roared, the booming proclamation scaring the bejesus out of everyone in the restaurant and breaking several glasses on Aunt Melba's counter. She fluttered out the door as some new customers walked in.

I waited a few minutes inside Aunt Melba's Country Kitchen to make sure Phyllis the talking bug, and apparently a woman with whom I had been involved at some time in my past, wasn't waiting outside to ambush me and crawl back into my ear. As I sat there pretending to finish my now cold coffee, I smiled sheepishly and nodded my head at the other customers. What else could a man do after having just been publicly cussed at and humiliated by an extremely overwrought bug?

(From the novel *Invasion of the Moon Women* by James Wharton)

HANKY-PANKY

Maureen the Adulterous Goldfish
(From the Case files of Private Investigator
Edmond Muncheman.   Case # 06147)

"No, Mr. Muncheman, I've never had thoughts of killing
my husband," said Olivia Morgenkrass. She paused for a
moment. "Alright, maybe I thought about it once or twice. Is
that such a bad thing? Doesn't everyone think about killing
their husband at one time or another?"

Private Investigator Edmond Munche was listening to the
woman spill out her story. He had heard many stories over his
long career and this was like all the rest.

"I'm very suspicious of my husband, you see," she
continued. "I'm sure he's having an affair but, I can't prove it.
And, that's where you come in. I want you to find the
evidence that will prove I'm right so I can divorce him."

Muncheman shook his head sympathetically. "I
understand, Mrs. Morgenkrass," he reassured her. "I'll get on
it right away. I will need a key to your house so I can set up
cameras. In case he brings his girlfriend home, we'll have him

on tape." Olivia Morgenkrass handed the P.I. Edmond Muncheman the key to her home.

"Oh, he'll bring her home alright. He already has," Olivia said.

"You didn't tell me about that Mrs. Morgenkrass," he said, wondering why the woman hadn't mentioned that important detail. "How do you know he brought the girlfriend home?"

"Two days ago," Olivia began, "I sat down at my make-up table and one of my lipsticks was open and lying on its side. Someone had used it. Only my husband and I live in our house, and unless he's taken to wearing make-up, someone else borrowed my lipstick."

"I see," replied Muncheman, pondering whether her husband might be partial to wearing lipstick or was dumb enough to bring his girlfriend to his wife's house. "Maybe he did both," Munche thought. "Everybody's nuts these days."

"And there's something else," Olivia said. "There were a few drops of water by the tube of lipstick, just little drips, you see. I never drip water on my make-up table. "It's the sacred place, you know."

"Yes, of course," answered Muncheman, a woman's make-up table is never to be disturbed by anyone." Muncheman was thinking of how tired he was being a private investigator. In this job, you always deal with the downside of humanity, he reflected. His list of cases over thirty years included affairs, scams, divorces, spying on wives for jealous husbands and vice versa. He'd even investigated a couple of murders and kidnappings. One guy insisted his wife was abducted by a UFO. Muncheman concluded she actually was abducted by a UFO and taken to another planet. He had to fight the guy in court to get the balance of his fee because he couldn't get the wife back for the guy.

Some guys would pay to have their wives abducted by UFO's. He had a whole list of names of men who would do just that. "Remember," one of them had told him, "if you ever run into a UFO, I'll pay you a straight $25,000.00 in cash to get her on board and taken to a galaxy far, far away." He wished he could make contact with some space aliens. He would be a rich man and life would be so much easier. Mrs. Morgenkrass' case was just another one of those nasty marriage gone bad situations. It wouldn't be a whole lot of trouble but he was just tired of dealing with all of it.

The next day Muncheman drove to the Morgenkrass house in his "Harry's Plumbing" truck. He also wore his "Harry's Plumbing" overalls. The neighbors would think he was visiting the house to do some plumbing repairs. Of course, the truck was not a plumbing repair truck, but a high tech surveillance vehicle loaded with the latest in electronic spyware. Muncheman decided to put only one camera in the living room of the house because everyone coming into the front door had to walk through the living room to access the rest of the house. The most noticeable feature of the living room was an enormous aquarium lavishly decorated with every manner of sea creature, castles, and other "fish toys" for lack of a better description. There was one absurdly large goldfish swimming in the aquarium.

That was how case # 06147 began two weeks earlier. However, it hadn't taken Muncheman long to uncover some important incriminating facts. He called Olivia Morgenkrass earlier that morning and she had just arrived.

"Good morning, Mrs. Morgenkrass," he said, as the attractive brunette sat down across the desk from him.

"Good morning, Mr. Muncheman," she replied. "You mentioned in your phone call you had some important information for me."

"Yes, I do, Mrs. Morgenkrass. I found out your husband is definitely having an affair."

"I knew it," Olivia replied. "I knew he was seeing another woman. And, she had the nerve to use my most expensive lipstick. I'm furious about that," she said, in an irritated voice. "Well, let's have it. Who is he seeing? Do I know her?"

Muncheman hesitated to answer. He looked at Mrs. Morgenkrass for several moments and then spoke. "Mrs. Morgenkrass, I don't wish to be indelicate but, we have an unusual situation here."

"Well, what is it?" Olivia asked excitedly.

"It's not what you think, Mrs. Morgenkrass," he said.

"What do you mean?" she asked. "Is he or is he not having an affair?"

"Oh yes, he's having an affair. But, the issue is with whom he's having the affair."

"For Pete's sake," said Olivia. "Just tell me who it is. I promise not to be surprised."

"Oh, but you will be surprised, Mrs. Morgenkrass," Muncheman countered.

"Stop playing games, Mr. Muncheman. Obviously, I'll be shocked by who he's having the affair with, but I want to know who it is. Has he got a boyfriend? Is that why he used my lipstick? Is he sleeping with his sister, his mother? Tell me, will you. You're driving me nuts."

Muncheman hesitated again. Olivia rolled her eyes, and rotated her hands one over the other as in "get on with it."

Muncheman looked at Olivia, an ominous expression on his face. "Mrs. Morgenkrass," he said, "your husband is having an affair with his goldfish Maureen."

"What!" exclaimed Olivia. "Is this some kind of joke? Did my cheating husband pay you more than I'm paying you so he could mess with my head?"

"I have pictures, Mrs. Morgenkrass, and videos. "I'll show them to you," Muncheman replied.

Two hours later Olivia Morgenkrass paid Muncheman his fee. She was numbed by what she had seen. "I never thought a man could have sex with a goldfish," she said, still shocked. "I also can't believe Maureen the goldfish would do this to me. I thought she liked me. I guess you can't trust anyone, can you?" Muncheman nodded that he agreed.

Can't I report him to the animal protection people or something?" she asked Muncheman.

"Well, technically, he hasn't broken any laws. The only time your husband came into contact with Maureen was when he put your lipstick on her lips. It was obvious both Maureen the goldfish and your husband had some type of liaison however they never came into physical contact during these sexual episodes. It was more of a Platonic union and any attorney could successfully argue they never had actual sex, even though they did. It was more of a telepathic sexual union. No, legally, I'm afraid he's home free. However, you can probably still get your divorce because the civil court has a lower standard of proof than the criminal court.

"Alright," said Olivia, as she walked out of Edmond Muncheman's office.

Muncheman made his final notes and stamped the file "Case Closed."

Unfortunately, two weeks later, Olivia Morgenkrass was again sitting in Edmond Muncheman's office. She was crying.

"Mr. Muncheman," she said, "remember that last day we met here in your office?" Muncheman nodded. "Anyway, when I left here I was infuriated. I rushed home and screamed at Maureen for ruining my marriage. I got my husband's little fish net out and scooped Maureen out of the aquarium. As I was carrying her toward the toilet, her little fish lips were pleading, 'No, Olivia, Please no!' I'll never forget the look on her goldfish face. Anyway, I threw Maureen into the toilet and flushed it. She tried desperately to swim against the swirling current but it was no use. Her goldfish body, though rather large, disappeared down the drain. It was too horrible to contemplate."

"Well, I can see why that would upset you, Mrs. Morgenkrass. It's too bad you didn't give Maureen to a neighbor. Try to forget the whole thing," Muncheman added, which was the only thing he could think to say.

"I tried to," said Olivia. "But, I have an even bigger problem."

"What's that?" asked Muncheman, hoping he could end the conversation and get to his favorite bar and have a martini or three.

"My husband has filed for divorce because I told him I murdered Maureen," she answered.

"Isn't that what you wanted?" asked Munche.

"Yes, of course," Olivia replied. "But that's not my problem."

"Then what is your problem?" asked Muncheman, on the verge of losing his patience and quitting the private investigator business forever.

"Maureen's back," replied Olivia. "She's haunting the hell out of me."

"What?" Muncheman asked. In all the years he'd been in business, he'd never heard of anyone being haunted by a dead goldfish.

"It's true," insisted Olivia. "Every day, I find that same tube of lipstick opened and drops of water next to it. I even found a fish scale on my lip when I used that lipstick. Every night I see Maureen swimming through the room. She glows a bright gold. She always stops at the foot of my bed and looks at me. Her lips move like when she and my husband did when they were, well you know, having that weird sex. You've got to help me, Mr. Muncheman."

Muncheman looked at the distraught woman. "Mrs. Morgenkrass, the paranormal is a bit out of my area of expertise. I investigated a flying saucer incident one time and that didn't go very well. I don't think I can do you much good in a goldfish haunting. However, I'll refer you to someone I know, alright."

Olivia shook her head. "Fine," she said.

She returned home later that day and walked into her bedroom. "Hello Olivia," a ghostly voice greeted her. "I'm over here at the make-up table. I've tried all your lipsticks and just can't find the right shade."

The Seduction

My name is Dr. Milford Glans and my area of expertise is the paranormal. I hold the only Doctoral Degree ever awarded in Ghost Petology. You might wonder how I became interested in such a field. That is a strange story in itself. In 1997, I was working on my doctoral dissertation in the remote jungles of Thaga Thaga, a Fourth World country located on the African continent. I was studying the dietary habits of a very ancient tribe called the Mofugas. That the people of this tribe were very ancient also told me they were very old. What were they eating that enabled them to live so long?

However, I soon lost interest in trying to answer that question because they produced an extremely intoxicating beer called Woo Woo Jambi. I'd never gotten as drunk as I did that first night I drank it. One thing led to another and I married the chief's ninety-three year old widowed mother. I was twenty-four at the time.

I remember absolutely nothing about this night. By the way, I immediately filed for divorce when I became sober three days later. But, I was forced to live with the Mofugas for nine months until the tribe was certain my bride had not gotten pregnant on our honeymoon. It was also during this time that I discovered two remarkable things about the Mofugas.

First, they have incredible mind control, and because of this, they rarely find it necessary to go to war with their neighbors. You see, when Mofuga warriors line up on the battlefield, they have no weapons. However, using their mental prowess, they are able to move certain parts of their bodies from one location to another.

As an example, in one battle I witnessed a line of one hundred Mofuga warriors separated into groups of ten. As the Mofugas stood glaring at the enemy, each group of ten warriors simultaneously proceeded to move a particular body part to a different location on their bodies. Group one moved their noses from the front of their faces down to their left knees. Group two moved their ears down to their belly buttons. Group three moved their unmentionable reproductive organs to their foreheads. This continued until all ten groups had completed their particular body part migrations.

Then all one hundred warriors jumped up and down dancing and chanting and pointing to their newly relocated organs. The enemy tribe figured the Mofugas had some kind of spiritual power or black magic and threw down their spears and ran away screaming in terror. It was a great victory for the Mofugas, the only mishap being the chief's son was unable to relocate his unmentionable reproductive organ from his forehead back to its original location.

At first, the chief's son was uncomfortable with this situation. He was especially frustrated when he walked because his unmentionable sexual organ hanging from his forehead swung back and forth in front of his eyes like a windshield wiper on a car. However, on a trip to New York, he realized almost no one noticed this minor biological discrepancy. The only exception was the noted designer Pablo DeCrona who has incorporated this design into his women's hats collection titled, "Head Bob," which will debut at the Paris show later this year.

But, I got off the second remarkable thing about the Mofugas which is the more important subject. The Mofugas also have a very healthy relationship with the dead, especially their deceased pets. That's when I learned that our pets never really leave us. You see, when pets die, they simply move to a different location in our dimension, much like the Mofugas' noses when they migrate to another position on their bodies. This allows our pets to return from the dead and comfort us or save us from harm. They also come back to take their revenge if they were mistreated. And that's how I became interested in the science of Ghost Petology.

There was however, a sad but irritating footnote to my story. My marriage of nine months to my ninety-three year old wife was not a union made in heaven. Unfortunately, it would best be described as quite the opposite. For the entire nine months, she accused me of seducing her and getting her pregnant. She and her two badly overweight dogs, Waugogi and Shakespeare (don't ask) constantly chased me around the village, she, brandishing a stick and screaming at the top of her lungs, and the dogs barking their fool heads off (don't I wish).

On the final day of my nine months of marital bliss, she passed away. Both dogs dropped dead within the hour. It turned out she wasn't pregnant. Luckily, the dogs' death released me from the responsibility of adopting them. The Mofuga chief then informed me I could leave the village, admonishing me to never to return because I had a "lecherous streak." He also ordered me to get help with my problem, as he put it.

I promised I would never return and would seek counseling for my lustful nature. I thought it was over and done with and I was never so happy to return to New York. I completed my degree and opened my Ghost Pet counseling business. It thrived immediately and I am now a noted authority on Ghost Pets.

About six months after I opened my business, however, I myself encountered a bizarre problem concerning "ghost pets." Unfortunately, a much bigger problem accompanied my initial plight. As I was the only expert in the field of Ghost Petology, I had no one to turn to for help. It was a problem I had to solve by myself. To this day, nearly ten years later, I have been unable to resolve my predicament.

The conundrum is this. My ninety-three year Mofuga wife's dogs, Waugogi and Shakespeare have returned to haunt me. They chase me around my office, snarling, snapping and generally being a great nuisance. What is more unfortunate, however, is that my Mofuga wife came along with them. She starts off each haunting by whacking me on the back with her "husband stick," as she refers to it. Then Waugogi nips me in my ankle. For some reason, Shakespeare isn't as hostile as the other two members of the ghostly trio. I actually think he's taken a liking to me, although he still barks and growls, putting on his obligatory good show for the other two, I suppose.

It is, of course, extremely embarrassing when I jump up in the middle of a session with a client and begin running around my office dodging invisible dogs and a ninety-three year old ex-wife smiting me with her "husband stick." Frankly, it frightens my clients to see me unable to vanquish my own ghost pet problems. They wonder how I can help them when I obviously have my own "demons" to fight. And that's not to mention the hefty fee I'm charging them for my advice. My credibility is zero at that point.

I never married, of course. I came close to getting engaged several times, but after a number of embarrassing incidents at restaurants, one of which ended up getting me arrested, women have steered clear of me. My ninety-three year old ex-wife even appeared in the bedroom of one of my girlfriends one night. She had her two intimidating dogs with her and, in the Mofuga manner, was naked from the waist up.

"Her boobs hung down past her belly button," the poor girl told me. "And she kept screaming, 'Him my man. Him my man.' Then she whacked me with her 'husband stick.' What the hell is a husband stick?" my girlfriend asked me.

I never saw her again.

I don't know the answer to my problem and probably never will. I thought about changing my name and going into hiding someplace. But, in my experience, the ghost pets always find you. There is no place to hide, as the saying goes.

On the other hand, "I'm beginning to like Shakespeare. He's only bitten me one time. I think he likes me too. No, really.

Hanging Samuel Greeley

"You have any last words, Samuel Greeley?" the heavy-set, bearded man asked. "If not, as the duly elected judge of Beckett County, I rule the hanging shall proceed."

"Well, Judge Marmsley," Samuel Greeley replied as he looked down at the crowd from the back of his horse, "I was thinkin' maybe we could all calm down a bit and think this thing through in a way what might have a more promisin' outcome fer me."

"We want to be rid of the likes of you," Judge Marmsley countered. The crowd cheered in agreement.

"But judge, all I done was steal one ugly cow. That hardly qualifies as rustlin'. Rustlin' is when a whole bunch of cowboys ride out of the hills with six guns blazin' and shootin' other cowboys and steal a million or so cows. That's rustlin'."

"I don't need a varmint like you providin' me with the legal definition of rustling," Judge Marmsley replied. "Let the hangin' go forward."

"Wait, judge," a voice in the crowd cried out, just as Willard Thomas raised his hand to slap the condemned man's horse and send Samuel Greeley into the hereafter.

"Who shouted out?" Judge Marmsley asked.

"It was me, your honor," the voice answered.

"Step forward so I can see who you are," an irritated Judge Marmsley hollered. He was annoyed because he wanted to get over to the saloon and celebrate the hangin', which of course he couldn't do until there had actually been one. And the hangin' in progress wasn't making much progress.

The spectators stepped aside and made a path through the middle of the crowd so the person who called out could reach the front and present himself to the judge. There was a collective gasp from the crowd as a cow walked past them toward the judge who was standing on the elevated platform at the front of the crowd.

Samuel Greeley, sitting on his horse six paces from the judge, nervously peered out at the crowd. Willard Thomas, swatting flies with his hat, stood at the rear of the horse waiting for the signal to whack the animal's back-side and put an end to Samuel Greeley.

"What's that cow doin' down there?" the visibly aggravated judge inquired to the crowd in general. No one answered.

"Is this some kind of joke?" the judge asked. Again, no one answered.

"I was the one who interrupted the hanging," a voice said. "Everyone, including the judge, looked toward the cow which seemed to be where the words were coming from.

"I know it's a little unusual to see a talking cow, judge," the voice said. It was now abundantly obvious that it was indeed the cow that was speaking. Again, the crowd gasped. So did the judge.

"Are you indeed addressing me?" the judge asked as he looked directly at the cow.

"Yes, your honor, I am," the cow replied.

"How is it you have the ability to speak, ma'am or is it mister?" Judge Marmsley asked.

"That would be a rather confusing story, judge," the cow answered. "And it's ma'am, if you don't mind."

"Well, I'm sure we'd all like nothing better than to hear about that, ma'am" the judge replied.

"Actually, I'd much rather be enjoyin' a cold beer and a shot," a voice protested from the front row of spectators.

"Shut up, Mose," the judge ordered. "You'd rather be enjoyin' a cold beer and a shot anytime and today is no exception." The crowd laughed perfervidly (look it up, ha, ha), always appreciative of Judge Marmsley's biting wit.

"I'm allowing you to continue ma'am, but with the proviso your story ties into your objection to the hanging proceeding," the judge replied. "With that understanding, please resume, ma'am," the judge said.

"Thank you, judge," the cow responded. "How I came to be a speaking cow absolutely relates to the hanging. You see, I am actually dead, judge." The crowd gasped again.

"You're the gaspingest crowd I ever encountered," the judge scolded. "Stop your gasping so we can get on with this distressing affair."

"What I mean, judge, is not that I as a cow am dead. You see, my cow body is alive. However, and this is where it gets tricky, my cow soul is actually from my dead human body."

"What the hell are you talking about, madam?" the judge gasped. "Don't gasp, judge," the crowd uniformly reminded Judge Marmsley. Their admonition to the judge sounded so authoritative, the crowd collectively decided, they thought it would be right clever to re-issue their warning. "Don't gasp, judge," they said again. The warning advanced to a chant, "Don't gasp, judge. Don't gasp, judge."

"Stop that," the judge ordered, seeing that the crowd was becoming restless. The crowd quieted.

"Please ma'am, if you will go on," the judge instructed the cow.

"Thank you, judge. To explain all this, you need to understand that I used to be a human and married to Samuel Greeley."

"You were Mrs. Samuel Greeley?" the judge asked.

"Yes, judge, I was. Unfortunately, I was not a good wife, the cow said," beginning to weep.

"She had a rovin' eye," Samuel Greeley blurted hoarsely. "It's hard talkin' with this noose around my neck, yer honor," he added.

"Shut up," the judge replied.

"I fell in love with Samuel's best friend," she explained. "Unfortunately, when we were driving out of town, we ran into a train."

"You mean you had to stop at a train crossing?" the judge asked.

"No, my boyfriend was at the wheel and he was a terrible driver. We actually ran into the train in broad daylight. I got killed but he didn't. Ain't that the way it always is?" Mrs. Greeley, the cow asked. "It's never the dumb driver, always the passenger that gets killed," she said, answering her own question.

"I'm not sure I understand," the judge said.

"Duh! I was killed when my boyfriend drove his car into a train. My human body passed away so my spirit had to find a new home. So I found this accommodating cow."

"That ain't completely true," Samuel Greeley objected. It's true she got killed, but she didn't have to inhabit a cow's body. She could have gone anywhere."

"I came here to this cow's body to be near Samuel," the cow replied weeping. "I realized I still loved him, even though I was dead. Besides, he's a good driver, not like that idiot friend of his. He ought to choose smarter friends, don't you think, judge."

"I don't want to get involved in your marital problems," Judge Marmsley replied. "Just tell me why we shouldn't hang your estranged husband."

"Samuel wasn't rustling cattle when he stole me. That's why. He was just taking me away with him so we could discuss our problems privately."

"I see," the judge replied. "But, as a cow, you are owned by the Bar Seven Ranch. That means your husband was stealing livestock from them. You're just a spirit inhabiting the cow's body."

"Not so, judge," the cow Mrs. Greeley replied. "My spirit now inhabits this cow body, but if I leave, the cow dies. A dead cow ain't gonna' do the Bar Seven Ranch any good. Under these circumstances, I'm a free person, cow rather, and can come and go as I please."

"I'll need to check the statute on that," Judge Marmsley replied.

"I already did," Mrs. Greeley the cow said. "Article 7, section 21, paragraph 6 of the state laws regarding livestock states: 'If a human spirit comes to be in possession of a cow's body, that cow is no longer considered to be livestock. It is now a human and can come and go as it pleases.' But, I'm sure you are knowledgeable of that already, judge, being as well-versed on the law as you are."

"Ahem, well uh, yes, Mrs. Greeley, of course I am."

"Well, good," Mrs. Greeley said, smiling. "If someone will kindly remove the rope from Samuel's neck, he and I shall be on our way."

Judge Marmsley nodded to the executioner Willard Thomas, who was furiously waving his hat swatting flies.

"Yahoo!" exclaimed Thomas, who was so happy he joyfully swiped his hat at one last fly. Unfortunately the fly was resting on the horse's rear end, and in a fatal miscue, when Willard's hat whacked the fly it simultaneously whacked the horse which immediately charged forward. Samuel Greeley was left hanging in the air, his body swinging back and forth like a pendulum.

"Samuel Greeley was my best friend," Willard yelled mournfully. I didn't even want to be his executioner, except the job paid so well. But, I didn't mean to kill him."

They cut Samuel down right away and miraculously, he was still alive. The talking cow, Mrs. Greeley, walked over to

144

where Samuel Greeley sat on the ground rubbing his neck. "You almost got me killed you ugly old cow," he yelled.

"The cow turned and looked at Judge Marmsley. "See why I left him for his best friend, judge."

"Yeah," the judge answered. "I'd have left him too."

It had been a strange day, everyone decided, and the crowd disbursed and went their separate ways. Samuel Greeley got his horse back and he and his cow bodied wife left town, followed by Willard Thomas, the would-be executioner.

They became the best of friends, it was reported, until Willard ran off with Mrs. Greeley.

Samuel Greeley remarked that this development reminded him of the ancient Chinese riddle:

Question: What's the difference between a duck?

Answer: One leg's the same.

Danged imponderable.

About the Author

James Wharton was born in St. Louis, Missouri and traces his lineage to the Revolutionary War and Valley Forge. Wharton worked three years as a page in the U.S. Capitol in Washington, spent four years in the military, one in the Viet Nam War, attaining the rank of Captain. Wharton is an Adjunct Professor of Economics and Marketing. He attended Capitol Page School in the Library of Congress and graduated from Washington University in St. Louis. He has published five novels and five short story collections. He recently won three writing awards for short stories.

21542093R00084

Made in the USA
San Bernardino, CA
29 May 2015